I0687236

Luke's Gold

by

JoMarie DeGioia

PUBLISHED BY:

Bailey Park Publishing

Luke's Gold

Book One of the
Braunachs of the Dell Series

by

JoMarie DeGioia

Prologue

Cornwall, England

The present

Brianna Wellbrook stroked her little sister's hair, holding back her tears. And frustration. "There there, Violet."

Violet moaned softly and burrowed deeper into the pillow. The child looked so much younger than her seven years. Her cheeks were pale, her body impossibly small in her purple nightgown. Brianna brushed back a thin strand of Violet's golden hair and tucked it behind one ear. That ear showed the hint of a point, proof of their Pixie heritage. Their magic. Brianna whispered a curse. What good was Pixie magic when the family couldn't make Violet whole and well again?

For two long months Violet had worsened. For weeks now Brianna had watched her go from a bubbly little girl who merrily used her magic to this wan child who hardly laughed any more.

Violet's pretty pink bedroom, once the scene of happy disarray, now seemed austere. The white wooden bed faded from view with no shirts, pants or dresses draped over it. Stuffed animals sat in rows on the floor, ready for Violet to make them dance and move as if alive. Books waited to turn their pages at Violet's whim, eager to capture the little girl's nimble mind. Brianna dashed her hands over her face to wipe the wetness from her cheeks. Damn it, what could she do?

Nothing the Pixies tried had worked, not Christian prayers or ancient words. Brianna wouldn't give up hope. She'd been like a mother to Violet for the past five years, from when they'd lost their parents soon after Brianna's eighteenth birthday. Well, she wouldn't lose her sister. She couldn't.

"Please, God." Brianna closed her eyes and prayed softly. "Please don't take Violet, too."

For one selfish moment she gave in to the tears, to the feeling of impotence, as she wrapped her arms around her middle. The books on the shelves tumbled to the floor in a clattering rush. She opened her eyes and glanced at the mess.

"Come away from her, Brianna," Grandmother said.

Brianna wiped her tears away before turning toward her grandmother standing in the doorway.

She dropped a kiss on Violet's cheek and straightened. "I just wish…" Anger filled her again. "Oh, what good is a wish?"

Grandmother shook her head. "Now, love, don't feel that way. We haven't done everything. Not yet."

Brianna's heart raced at her grandmother's words and she hurried to her side. "What is this? Oh, please tell me there's a spell or glimmer we haven't tried, Grandmother. Is it strong enough to heal her?"

Her grandmother looked away, her mouth set. "No," she said. "There's nothing so simple as that, I'm afraid."

"Simple?" Brianna brushed her hair back from her face and snorted. "Oh, I don't dare hope for 'simple.'"

Grandmother smiled, the expression slight. "Come, love." She put her arm around Brianna's shoulders and urged her out of Violet's room and toward the parlor. "We have to hurry if we're going to save your sister."

Afraid to hope there was an answer, Brianna sat beside her grandmother on the settee. She saw little of the cozy room. The house seemed less alive now, the pall of Violet's illness leeching the life out of their home. Even her grandmother seemed less vibrant since Violet took ill.

Brianna twisted her hands in her lap as she closed her eyes, her damp lashes brushing her cheeks. Her stomach churned. "Please tell me what we can do, Grandmother. I don't know what I'd do if I lost her."

"Don't think it, Brianna." Grandmother rubbed Brianna's shoulders, easing some of the tension that thrummed through her. "I lost your mother. I only wish we didn't have to take this step. It could be dangerous."

"What step?" Brianna open her eyes, forcing back the urge to latch on to her Grandmother's cashmere-covered arm and give her a shake. "I don't care about the danger, Grandmother. Tell me. Please."

"I didn't want to do this, love. I didn't want you to take this step." After a long moment, her grandmother faced her. "I made a vow to keep my girls safe and I will."

Brianna heard the steel in the woman's voice, steel she wished she had a portion of to get Violet through this. She studied Grandmother's dear face then. She could see her past and her future in that face, could see her little sister in her grandmother's clear blue eyes.

"Tell me, Grandmother," Brianna said. "Tell me what I can do."

Her grandmother nodded and told Brianna a tale of stolen gold and a crystal key. Of a curse forged centuries ago. And a way to possibly heal Violet for good. Her words stunned Brianna. Could it work? Violet's faint moan came from her bedroom. It had to.

Chapter 1

Meath Province, Ireland 1810

"The lass was merely askin' me the time, Patrick," Sean MacDonald said.

"Leigh wasn't talkin' to you at the dance, Sean." Patrick MacDonald threw down his polishing rag. "Luke, tell him 'twas me the lass was wantin'. And for more than the time."

"'Tis not my concern, Patrick." Luke smiled at his brothers. "You and Sean worry it out."

Patrick glared at Sean and said nothing. Then he grinned and nudged him hard with his shoulder and the younger brother laughed.

"Leigh's sister is bonny," Sean said.

Luke laughed to himself. He and his brothers ran the shop together, their work valued by those in the dell and beyond. Shoemakers by trade and enchanted Braunachs by birth, the MacDonalds were known for their keen minds and their charm, able to sway mortals and Faery to their will with little more than a grin and glimmer.

Luke was the oldest at twenty-seven, but sometimes

he felt older still. No lass in the dell drew his heart, not Leigh or her bonny sister surely, and he began to wonder if he'd ever find a girl who wanted him for himself and not his MacDonald charm or fit body. Or his gold.

Luke set aside his work and cleaned off his bench. "I'll see you lads at Uncle's, then."

The sun slanted through the trees to the west as Luke walked down the wide cobblestone street that formed the center of their dell. Cozy houses and tidy shops were on either side and Luke nodded greetings to folks he'd known for years. The dell felt safe this spring evening. Then again, no dark magic ever came close enough to do much damage.

As he turned down the lane toward his uncle's cottage, he anticipated the coming evening. Ah, Mrs. O'Grady would serve up a hearty meal followed by her delicious biscuits. And after dinner, Uncle Seamus would tell his stories. Those tales drew Luke as much as the fine food.

As he neared the house, Luke heard a crash from within.

"Luke!" his uncle shouted.

Luke ran into the house and found his uncle sitting in the drawing room. White-faced, Seamus clutched the arms of the chair he sat in. Luke glanced at Mrs. O'Grady and the woman shook her head in confusion.

He looked back at Uncle Seamus. "What is it, Uncle?"

"She took it, Luke." Seamus grabbed Luke's hand and squeezed. "She took the gold."

Alarm shot through Luke. The gold?

"Who, Uncle?" he asked. "Pray, who took the gold?"

His uncle turned his eyes toward Luke. As Luke watched, the man changed. His eyes went vacant in his face, his mouth, slack. "I'm sorry, lad."

***

"What can I do?" Luke muttered as he set the shoe aside. How could he work when his family was in trouble? He wiped his hands on a cloth and sighed. Sunlight streamed into the workshop, falling over the cluttered, dusty room. His brothers hadn't worked in days, but Luke couldn't blame them.

Something must be done to heal his uncle. To make things right. It was his job, damn it. He had to be the one to fix this mess. He threw down the cloth. What could he do now?

"I know where the gold be, MacDonald," a low voice said from behind him.

Luke straightened and turned from his workbench. Daniel O'Shey perched on a stool beside the door, his black eyes gleaming just beyond a shaft of sunlight.

Luke folded his arms across his broad chest and glared down at the Leprechaun from the Ulster Province. "And how do you know this, O'Shey?"

Daniel's round face wore a distasteful grin. "Wot difference that be makin', MacDonald?" He winked. "I... persuaded the Cornish Pixies to tell me where she took the gold."

Luke could imagine the tactics the little imp had employed. Ulster Leprechauns weren't known for their cunning or their kindness. Luke was tempted to use his Braunach charm on Daniel, to bend him to his will, but he couldn't take the risk of sending him away before he revealed all of it. Damn it, he needed the information O'Shey possessed. He had to keep his emotions in check. For Uncle Seamus.

Luke took a deep breath. "What do you want, O'Shey?"

The little man's eyes glittered and Luke knew the answer.

"Me share," Daniel said. "When ya' find the Pixie, ya' give me a share o' the gold."

Luke weighed his request for a moment. His uncle needed the gold. But surely not all of it. He would worry about that later, when he had the gold in his hands.

He nodded at the Leprechaun. "Where?"

Daniel chortled. "The question be that, 'tis true." He hopped down off the stool and sauntered so close Luke could smell the swamp on his wrinkled clothes. "But ya' must also ask, 'when?'"

Luke spat out a string of curses. A time jump. There was only one man able to assist Luke's leap to recover the gold: the very one whose diminishing mind needed it so desperately. Uncle Seamus.

The theft of the gold meant more to the MacDonalds than a loss of wealth. Luke had to recover it, and he needed his uncle's amber pendant to accomplish that. A time jump, though? Resignation soured his belly.

"*When* then, you filthy imp?" Luke asked.

Daniel scowled, an ugly expression on his round face. He crossed his thick, short arms. "Maybe I won't be tellin' ya'!"

Luke grabbed him by his fat neck and held him aloft until Daniel's eyes bulged from his balding head.

"Okay," Daniel croaked. "I'll tell ya'!"

Luke dropped him to the floor. Daniel barely muttered the words he needed to hear before Luke tore out of the workshop, bound for his uncle's cottage.

He pulled open the door and rushed into the drawing room. "Patrick?" He slammed the door shut. "Patrick, damn it!"

Patrick stepped into the room, dragging his hands over his face. "Aye, Luke," he grumbled. "I'm here."

Patrick's clothes were rumpled and if Luke didn't miss his guess they were the same ones he'd had on the day before. Luke knew his brothers felt their uncle's illness keenly, but Patrick's appearance struck him as strange.

"What the devil ails you, brother?" Luke asked.

Patrick's blue eyes widened a fraction before his

gaze slid away from Luke. "I... I did not sleep well last night."

Luke could read the exhaustion on his brother's face, in the lines around his mouth and the dullness of his skin.

"The nightmares again?" he asked.

Patrick began to shake his head, then lowered his gaze to the floor. He sank into one of the overstuffed chairs that flanked the stone hearth and rubbed his hand over the back of his neck.

"Patrick, what—?" He shook his head. "Nay. I don't have time for this." He glanced past his brother toward the bed chambers. "How is Uncle Seamus?"

"The same." Patrick glanced up again, his brows drawn together. "He's just starin' out the window, hummin' some tune to himself."

Leaving Patrick in the drawing room, Luke went in to see his uncle. Seamus lay there in his bed, looking half the man he was before. His face was no longer ruddy with good health, his eyes were no longer a deep green sparkling with knowledge and humor. Nay, those eyes stared right through Luke and he stifled a shiver.

"Uncle Seamus?" Luke stepped closer to the bed.

"'Tis I, Uncle. Luke."

Seamus said nothing as he turned to stare at the yard beyond his window. Luke swallowed hard and sat beside his uncle. "I know where the gold is, Uncle." He took Seamus's slack hand in his. "Your gold."

Seamus gave a start and pinned Luke with a gaze sharp and clear. "She took it, Luke. You must find it and bring it home."

Luke's heart pounded. This was his uncle as he knew him, strong and vibrant. "Aye, Uncle."

But Seamus turned away again, his green eyes clouded. He was gone so quickly that Luke could almost have imagined the man's impassioned words. That was it, then. Luke had no choice but to take the leap.

"I will bring back the treasure, Uncle," he whispered. "On my word as a Meath Braunach." His eyes burned with tears and his chest grew tight. "As a MacDonald."

He rose and returned to the drawing room. "There's a connection between Uncle Seamus and the gold, Patrick," he said. "I know it in my heart. The treasure must be recovered."

Patrick straightened. "How, pray?"

Luke raked his fingers through his hair. Nothing but the truth would serve now, a part of it any way. He didn't want to involve any innocent Pixies if he could help it, and Patrick had a temper to rival Daniel's. "O'Shey told me where the gold is."

"Nay," Patrick said. "Where?"

"The future, brother," Luke said. "A place called Indianapolis, in the Colonies some two hundred years from now."

Patrick just stared at Luke, his eyes wide. Then he gave a slow nod. "The amber."

Luke nodded with a jerk. "Aye, the amber. I've no interest in flying through space with only a thin slice of amber for protection. 'Tis the only way."

Patrick stood and placed his hand on Luke's shoulder. "Go, then, and be safe. We'll be fine 'til you come back with the gold."

Luke wrapped his brother in a rough hug then crossed to his uncle's wooden desk set in one corner of the room. A box set on the top held money from the different times their uncle had visited over the years.

Luke chose money which read "United States of America," printed a few years earlier than the one O'Shey had said. He shoved a large stack of the bills into his pocket then pulled open a tiny drawer set deep into one side of the desk. Inside rested the amber, a smooth pierced disk the size of a gold coin suspended on a strip of supple leather. He lifted it and, as a shaft of light struck it, the amber winked at him. A jolt shot through him and his hand shook. That had never happened before.

Luke tied the leather thong around his neck and dropped the amber down his shirt. The disk was cool as it settled against his skin. He gave Patrick a nod before stepping out of the cottage. Without another look behind him he headed into the woods, to the clearing in the forest.

To the future.

Chapter 2

Luke stood in the clearing, one hand clutching his uncle's amber. The stone felt smooth and warm against his palm now and he loosened his grip. He'd never used the pendant, had only heard Seamus's stories about his many trips to places and times far from Ireland, far from now. The amber had been in the MacDonald family as long as the gold, and Luke believed it could track the treasure. He prayed it would.

He heard a rustling in the trees to his left and turned to the sound but saw nothing but shifting shadows, the underbrush swaying in an unseen wind. The sun dappled the grass at his feet, a breeze crossed his face, and Luke closed his eyes. He reasoned a prayer wouldn't be out of place and prayed that God would keep his family safe. The Lord knew he'd take all the help he could get.

He gripped the amber tightly. "To the gold," he murmured.

A shock went through him. A rushing sound filled his ears and he felt the earth tremble beneath his booted feet. The earth began to spin, whirling until he was almost too dizzy to stand. His stomach clenched and then… nothing.

A blackness filled his senses, void of sound and light and sensation. In the next moment he found himself on his backside as the world tilted then righted itself. He opened his eyes and sucked in a great breath.

The first thing he noticed was the noise. Ungodly sounds all around him, sending his heart pounding. Luke scrambled to his feet and quickly stepped toward the building behind him. A man passing by shot him a curious look but continued on his way. He wore clothes Luke had never seen before, long breeches topped with a matching jacket that stopped just below his backside. A long neck cloth finished his dress, and Luke saw that most of the men hurrying past wore the same type of outfit. He glanced down at his own clothes and knew he'd draw attention if he stood here any longer.

The busy street stretched wide in front of him, filled with shiny carriages making their noisy way without benefit of horses. The smells that assailed him were sickening. No sweet grass or strong earth or horseflesh filled his nostrils, just a burning scent that caused him to cough.

Judging by the buds on the trees he reasoned it must be spring here, too. In the wide window of the building beside him he spied breeches and shirts like those the men here wore, along with softer looking clothes in pale grays and greens and blues. He felt in his pocket for the now money he'd taken from Seamus's stash. Still there. Blowing out a breath, he entered the store.

Luke took a moment to look around, pleased that the noise and smell of the street didn't linger when he let the glass door close behind him. Here he smelled sandalwood and the sharp sting of perfume.

"May I help you?" a feminine voice asked.

He turned to find a woman eyeing him. She wore a simple skirt of black with a shirt that looked like a man's, though it was tighter than a man would wear it and unbuttoned to reveal the tops of her breasts. As he watched, she arched her back and smiled. Luke swallowed in response. His charm worked on mortal women, then. Bloody wonderful.

"Aye, miss." He took a step away from her. "I be needin' some clothes."

"I see." The woman slowly ran her gaze over him.

"But I must say I like your costume. Very PBS."

He had no idea what she was talking about, but he nodded anyway. She showed him some of the breeches and waistcoats the dandies on the street wore. Instead, he walked toward a rack holding shirts made of plaids he'd never seen on any Scotsman.

He touched one shirt and found it as soft as if it had been washed over and over. "I like this."

The woman murmured agreement. "Oh, let me see if we have your size." She ran her hands over his shoulders and he stilled. "Nice, broad shoulders." As she walked toward the back of the store, her hips swayed.

Luke found a male clerk standing near a humming box on the counter and crossed to him. "I'd like breeches, please. Like the pale blue ones in the window."

The man blinked at him. "Breeches? Oh, jeans." He, too, ran his eyes over Luke but without the predatory gleam the salesgirl had shown. "Hmm. Thirty-two waist, I'd say," he said. "Maybe thirty-six length."

Luke shrugged. The man turned to the shelves behind him and pulled out a few pairs of the pants Luke had admired in the window. He handed them to Luke and he found that they, too, felt like they had been washed many times. "You can try them on in there," the clerk said.

The woman returned with the shirts and Luke took them and the pants into the small room the man indicated. The shirts were soft. The pants fit like a second skin and buttoned like his breeches. They wouldn't fit over his boots, though. He stood there in his bare feet and wondered what to do next.

"What about shoes, honey?" the woman asked.

Luke turned to see her feet beneath the edge of the swinging door. How long had she been standing there?

She entered the tiny room and he stepped back to allow as much space as possible between them.

She held up what looked like stockings. "I brought some socks." She looked down. "Big feet. Nice."

Luke felt her gaze move up to his groin and gave a small shake of his head. "I thank you, lass," he said.

She handed him the stockings and pressed closer. "Gerald won't bother us in here."

Luke placed his hands on her shoulders and gently eased her away from him. "The shoes, lass. Please."

"All right." She pouted as she turned away. "I'll find you something in a thirteen, I guess."

Luke rolled his eyes and pulled on the white stockings she brought for him. He picked up his old clothes and left the dressing room. When he came out he found the man, Gerald, waiting with a few pairs of shoes. The woman was nowhere to be seen, to Luke's relief. He didn't need the complication of a tryst, least of all with a mortal in another time.

Luke looked at the shoes, as fine as any he'd made in their shop at home. The colors! He picked up one of the white and blue shoes and grinned. "It's so light."

"Yes," Gerald said. "These sneakers are very popular. Cross-trainers."

Luke had no idea what he was talking about, but he had to have the shoes. He slipped on the sneakers and chose a pair of the green ones as well. Uncle Seamus loved all things green.

The man totaled Luke's purchases on the humming box at the counter. A few pairs of pants, several soft plaid shirts, plain buttonless shirts for "tea" the man said could be worn beneath the plaids, and the remarkable

25

sneakers. Luke went through the pocket of his old breeches and paid the man. Thankfully he'd taken plenty of Seamus's now money. To pay so much for clothes, though? His brothers would have a good laugh over this.

Luke thanked the man and took his bags. As he stepped back out onto the busy street he glanced about. Now what? His amber was cold and still beneath his new shirt, giving him no direction to find the thieving Pixie. He needed to rest after the time jump, and the jarring dose of the future hadn't ease his mind or body. His stomach growled. He had to have something to eat. He'd worry about where to sleep later.

Lining this main street of the city were plenty of places that served hearty food and stout ale. One looked much like a pub back in the dell, with dark woods and green-shaded lanterns, so he entered. He ignored the curious looks his manner of speaking drew and ordered some items by their intriguing pictures on the menu. The chicken wings cooked in piping-hot sauce stung his mouth and the things called "cheese fries" dripped an ungodly orange dressing that was salty and tangy. Oh, the food was nothing like Mrs. O'Grady made. He smacked his lips and grinned, drinking down two full mugs of ale to cool his mouth.

He put off leaving the pub as long as he could. Where would he go? The noisy street held no draw for him. He didn't want night to fall without having a place to sleep. He left enough money on the table to pay his bill and braced himself as he went back out onto the sidewalk.

That rustling sound came again, the shuffle of feet, and Luke turned to see nothing but more strangers hurrying past him. Strange. He lifted his head he sniffed the air. No ocean smell, he was disappointed to find. No lake that he could see. He saw a sign for the White River State Park and walked a few blocks toward the river. To his disappointment the White River bore little resemblance to its name. Brown and slow, it was unappealing. There were no places to stay beside it anyway. He turned from the river and continued down the sidewalk.

Thanking God for his quick Braunach mind, he set the noises and confusion of the city aside and focused on finding a place to settle. The sound of water drew him at last and he soon found himself near a fountain. Canals snaked away from it, manmade from smooth-hewn stone. Tall buildings stood near these canals, and one resembled an inn despite its height. Luke pulled open a wide glass door and stepped into what looked like a drawing room. Settees lined the walls and large floral arrangements colored the room.

Luke shifted his bags of clothes to one hand and stepped toward a long desk. "Excuse me."

The dapperly-dressed man behind the desk smiled up at him. "May I help you?"

"I need a place to stay for a short time, sir."

"For how long?" The man's brows drew together. "We don't lease by the night, but if you furnish references and pass a credit check we can do a month-by-month."

Luke had no time to furnish the references or credit checks the man mentioned, whatever those were. Surely some of his uncle's money and his own charm could secure a room. A gentle push would have the man seeing things Luke's way.

"That would be fine," Luke said.

The innkeeper escorted him to double doors made of some thick brass-colored metal. With the dinging of a bell the doors slid open and Luke glimpsed a small square room walled with glass within. The outside was visible through the glass walls and Luke looked at the man in question.

"The apartment is on the ninth floor, Mr. MacDonald," he said.

Luke didn't see any stairs in the glass room. The man stepped inside and looked at Luke expectantly. Luke got in just as the doors closed with a whoosh behind him, and he jumped as the little room began to shake. Suddenly his stomach fell to his feet as the glass box rose. He closed his eyes and willed his stomach to settle as his heart raced. When he opened them he found the manager watching him.

"Don't like heights, I take it?" the man said with a knowing smile.

Luke couldn't speak. Heights? He peered over the man's shoulder to see sky and clouds. What the devil..? His heart pounding, he turned to the double doors at his back. They opened with another of those little dinging sounds and after the innkeeper stepped out Luke took a tentative step out onto the carpet. Back on firm ground, thank the Lord. A long hallway stretched before him and he followed the other man past several paneled doors to stop in front of one of them.

"Ninety-two thirteen," the man read off the plaque next to the door.

Luke could only nod, his head still spinning after the flight in the glass box.

The man opened the door and waved an arm as he showed off the rooms. The flat was dull and drab with all the life of a February morning in Dublin.

"Here is the living room," the man said. "The bedroom is through that door. I think you'll find it very suitable for one man."

"Very," Luke answered. *Especially for one Braunach who didn't plan to be here long.*

"You have a full bath with a shower in there," the man went on. "And the kitchen is stocked with dishes and silverware. There isn't a washer and dryer but you can call the desk and we'll clean your clothes for a fee."

Luke nodded again, feeling like the biggest fool. A

shower? Was it raining in there? He didn't hear any water. The laundry he understood. Mrs. O'Grady looked after their domestic affairs in the dell; there was probably a housekeeper somewhere in this big building, too.

The man handed Luke two matching keys. He took a folded paper from his pocket and spread it out on the small round table near the kitchen. "Two months' rent, Mr. MacDonald," he said. "And security."

Security? Luke could use some right now. There was no way in Hell he'd step close to that large window behind the ugly beige settee.

"How much, then?" Luke asked.

The man named a large amount of money which Luke paid from his stash. The innkeeper arched a brow then grinned. "Corporate accounts are the best, huh?"

Luke doubted the man would pry into his affairs. He left several lines on the sheet blank and signed his name. Then he stared into the man's eyes and smiled. "I'm not from here. You can trust me to keep things as they are."

The innkeeper blinked, wiping his brow as he nodded. "Yes, yes." He glanced at the paper where Luke had scribbled his information. "Ireland?" the man asked.

"So you're a consultant, then."

Why not? "Aye," Luke said.

He stared at Luke for a moment before his eyes cleared. "Call the desk if you need anything, Mr. MacDonald."

With that, the man left Luke to his odd quarters. The cost had surprised Luke, and he hoped he'd be home before he had to pay more to the innkeeper. Security, the man had said. Well, Luke would have all the security he needed when he had his family's gold back in his hands.

He tossed his bags of clothes on the wide bed in the tidy bedroom and stretched out beside it. The day caught up to him in a rush. He recalled that odd rustling he'd sensed right before the leap but the time jump had worn him out. His mind was as tired as his body.

He wouldn't think about the ride up to his apartment in a glass box that rose faster than smoke from a pipe, causing his stomach to drop just as fast. He wouldn't think about the lass in the clothing store who had all but offered herself to him that afternoon. His head ached from using his charm and his wits since dropping into this strange place. He yawned. He'd look for the Pixie tomorrow. Tonight he'd sleep.

Chapter 3

In the morning Luke accustomed himself to the workings of marvels such as running water. *Hot* water! He was pleased to find with just the turn of a handle he could have steaming water to bathe with. This was surely the "shower" the innkeeper had mentioned. After a few tentative jiggles of the cold handle on the tall chamber pot, the sound of sucking water made him jump back. He did it again, watching the water swirl and swirl until it disappeared like before. He made use of the contraption, nodding with satisfaction when he sent the soiled water down into the hole. Interesting

Little bottles of cleansers were lined up beside the washbasin, and he opened the one marked "shampoo." Was that French? It smelled like spice and flowers, very nice. The bottle had a lot of long words on it, some that looked like Latin. One word on the label said "hair," so Luke took it into the washtub. The soap was easier to fathom and lathered generously in the stream of hot water pouring down. The shower was vastly preferable to washstands and pots and hauling buckets of water. He'd miss these conveniences when he went home.

Home. God, he missed the dell. And his family. He closed his eyes and let the water pound down on him. How was his uncle now? Did he even notice Luke was gone? Patrick and Sean were taking care of the old man in Luke's absence. He prayed that Patrick was up to the responsibility. Sean was too young to do more than worry.

Luke dressed in his modern clothes and laced up his sneakers. Nice. His stomach rumbled. He couldn't eat all his meals at the pubs that lined that busy street. That was certain. His uncle's money had to last until he found the bloody Pixie. Surely there was a market nearby. The innkeeper had shown him the cold box and the oven. Luke wouldn't touch the oven, but the cold box would hold the food he'd buy. He rubbed his hands over his face. Lord, there was so much to keep straight. He wanted to focus on finding the Pixie, not on learning to function in Indianapolis.

He took the keys the manager had given him and stepped out into the hallway. The up-and-down box was to his left. An elevator, Luke remembered the innkeeper had called it. He didn't look forward to stepping into that thing again. He saw a sign for the stairs and gladly walked down the nine flights to the lobby.

He stepped outside and lifted his head to sniff the morning air, finding it as stale and peculiar as yesterday. Keeping to the sidewalk, he made his way to the nearest market. The smell of coffee filled his nostrils and he couldn't resist entering a busy little restaurant. He stepped behind several people barking out odd combinations of words while loud machines behind the counter ground and gurgled. Skinny double shot no foam? Tall mocha with whip? The man standing in front of Luke wasn't as tall as he, and he carried no whip. Strange.

"Half caf toffee nut," the thin man behind the counter called.

Luke looked around for a cow and only saw a cup made of paper topped with a glossy white lid.

"Thanks," a woman said beside him. She reached for the cup smiled as she lifted it to her nose, wearing the same expression Seamus wore when he listened to his favorite songs. Or his brother Sean when Mrs. O'Grady set a platter of her special shortbread biscuits on the table. A pang of loneliness struck him.

"May I help you?" the man asked.

Luke glanced up at the board behind him, lost in the colored chalk and scrawled pictures.

"Hello!?" the man shouted.

"Coffee," Luke said.

"Just coffee?" the man asked.

"Aye."

Shrugging, the man quickly filled one of those paper cups and handed it to Luke. "Four dollars."

Luke pulled back. "Four dollars? For a cup of coffee?" That was nearly what he paid for his thick new stockings!

When the man just shrugged again, Luke stepped up to the chirping box like the one in the clothing store and paid the girl with pink hair standing behind it. Pink hair? Jewelry dangled from one eyebrow and twinkled on one side of her nose. Was she a Faery? When she bellowed out the next person's order, Luke made up his mind. The amber was cool and silent against his throat, so he guessed he was right. She was no Faery, just a brash American with peculiar taste in jewelry.

He left the place and sipped his coffee as he looked for a market. He didn't have to walk long before he found one crammed with all the items he would need for his short stay here. More of Seamus's money bought bread, fruit, vegetables and milk. He saw strange drinks in bottles of what looked like glass but were very light. The stuff bubbled like ale but looked like candy and there was no way he'd taste it. The Lord knew what it would do to his teeth.

He saw a box of cereal with the little man dressed in green, a Leprechaun even uglier than Daniel O'Shey. Well, Luke didn't need those particular charms of luck when he had his own charm and cunning. He chose instead a box with a smiling sea captain that made him think of the ports on the coast of Ireland.

After he returned to the apartment building and carried the bags of groceries up to his room, he walked slowly toward the wide window behind the ugly settee. He pulled aside the wheat-colored curtains. The city stretched out below him, drab and cluttered with only touches of green here and there. Why did anyone live here? The White River snaked in the distance.

Where was the Pixie? She hid well in this place, 'twas true. She had magic. He had nothing but his charm, his sharp mind and his uncle's money. And if he didn't find her soon, he'd have nothing but the guilt of failure bitter in his gut.

"Where are you?" He touched the amber but felt nothing other than smooth stone beneath his fingers. "Where the devil are you?"

***

Luke sat at the counter of the crowded coffee shop, happy to find it wasn't like the fancy shops that lined the streets of the city, filled with the sounds of conversations between mortals and unseen folk on small devices held near their ears.

Around each square table of the coffee shop sat four metal chairs with plump seats, and nearly all of them were occupied. The stool beneath Luke was also padded and comfortable and the place smelled like eggs and bacon and strong coffee.

What had drawn him into this place he couldn't recall, just an itch in the middle of his chest he could attribute to the thick air in the city. His amber shifted against his skin as a serving girl passed in front of him and he leaned his elbows on the long white counter.

He admired her trim figure as she bustled behind the counter. The tinkling of silverware and murmurs of conversation fell from his notice as he studied her. Oh, he didn't have to imagine the lush figure hidden beneath the snug and simple T-shirt, the round bottom caressed by her blue jeans. He almost preferred the close-fitting pants of this time to the dresses worn by the women of his. What would she look like in a sprigged day gown, her bosom teasingly displayed but the rest of her hidden beneath skirts and petticoats? Her small feet dressed in fine kid shoes made by a MacDonald instead of her simple canvas sneakers? Aye, she'd be a vision.

He shifted on the stool as his body reacted to her closeness. Again, the amber moved against his skin. In the five days he'd spent in this strange city he'd had offers from mortal women that would make his uncle blush. First the woman at the clothing store and then women on the street or in the pub, all reacting strongly to his Braunach charm. He didn't seek their attentions; it seemed he had no control over his charm here. Neither his body nor his mind had been affected by any one of those women, though. This girl caused his senses to sharpen and his body to tighten in his jeans. Why?

***

Brianna trembled as she set the coffee pot down. He'd found her. All the way from Ireland, he'd tracked her down in her snug little pocket of security. She'd expected it; Grandmother had told her as much. That the Braunach would be so tall and strong, though? *Grandmother, why didn't you warn me?*

She held her hands in fists tucked in the folds of her apron and turned away from him.

Another waitress came to stand next to her. "Something wrong, Bree?"

Brianna faced Lori, a woman she'd worked with nearly every day since coming to this place. Dark-haired and intense in both her scowls and smiles, Lori was different from anyone Brianna had known in Cornwall. The woman obviously considered her a friend, and that warmed Brianna's heart.

"Nothing's wrong, Lori." Brianna wiped her damp palms on the front of her jeans. "It's just been a busy morning."

Lori stared at her with that frankness so common to Americans and clicked her tongue. "Tell me if you need a break."

She left Brianna's side and walked further down the counter. Brianna wasn't as lucky. She kept herself as far from the Braunach as she could, watching him out of the corner of her eye as she waited on the customers around him. He seemed out of place as he talked with his mortal companion. The blond man had been in the shop a couple of times before, a friendly man who teased and flirted with her in that ease all Americans seemed to share. She'd felt no threat from him then and she didn't now. His companion, however? He was danger itself. She stifled another shiver.

The Braunach was striking. His brown hair, full of auburn streaks, was thick and wavy. He had a ruddy complexion that glowed with virility. Hale and bloody hearty, no doubt. He was large, and exuded strength. Yes, he was strong. And cunning, unless she missed her guess. Weren't all the blasted Braunach known for their bloody sharp minds?

When he'd stepped into the coffee shop she'd known; the floor had shifted beneath her feet. Oh, the Braunach charm. She could feel it in her blood, in the tingle over the surface of her skin. He was full of it. Would he try to charm her here? She trembled. Now?

Anger caused her cheeks to flush hot and her breath to hitch in her chest. The Braunach's charm was forgotten now. He could smile his beautiful smile and use those green eyes but she wouldn't surrender her mind or her will. And she wouldn't surrender her treasure either, damn him. It was hers, and dear to her heart. And she was damned if she'd turn it over to this Braunach!

Chapter 4

Luke eyed the pretty little lass, noting the smooth cheeks now flushed pink as she served her customers. She worked the humming machine at the end of the counter and deftly handled the customers' money. Her English accent was faint but he caught it and felt that itch in his chest again. She might be from now but she wasn't from *here*. He was certain of it.

The girl's hair, done in a fetching style gathered at the crown and swinging free to brush her shoulders, revealed her slender ivory neck. Her skin looked dewy fresh and smooth and his fingers itched to touch her. Her features were delicate, her face heart-shaped. She turned again, showing him her perfect profile. Did her ear show the slightest hint of a point? He focused fully on the girl. Her thick hair was straight and shiny in the overhead lamps, of as pure a gold as his uncle's treasure. His belly clenched and the amber disk suddenly grew warm against his throat. Nay, it couldn't be!

"You!" he said.

She whirled toward him and widened her eyes, eyes as blue as the sky above his beloved Ireland. Certainty

44

struck him hard in the gut, his simple lust for her gone in an instant. It was the Pixie, damn her to Hell.

The Pixie feigned confusion as she quickly ran her gaze over him before taking a step backward. Her little chin rose as she straightened her spine, affecting a casual air. He shook his head at her. Her affected innocence wouldn't keep him from the task that brought him through the years. Nay. He'd traveled leagues from his home to drop here in the middle of these strange Colonies. He wouldn't let her get away now.

He placed his fingers at the base of his throat. He fingered the smooth amber disk through his shirt and said a silent prayer of thanks to his uncle and to the Lord. The amber throbbed against his touch. The MacDonald clan knew much of the Cornish Pixies. Aside from their magic they held a dose of charm as well. Oh, perhaps not as strong as the Braunach. He didn't doubt this slip of a girl would be a formidable opponent. As the girl watched him, Luke slowly lowered his hand to the counter.

"May I help you, sir?" she asked.

"More coffee, pray," he said.

The lass arched one fair brow but served him. His

nostrils flared as she leaned closer. She smelled like fresh air and flowers. Again his body reacted and he clenched his hands in fists to keep from touching her. This place might lack the morals he'd been taught to respect, but even here and now a man didn't just touch any woman he fancied. His gaze fell to her T-shirt as she sucked in a breath. She was nicely formed. He didn't miss the tremble of her delicate hand as she held the glass pot above his thick china cup. He swallowed a smile. She wasn't immune to him, then.

She took a quick step back as if to escape him and his lips quirked. He raised the cup to his lips and blew gently to cool the coffee. She watched him and he couldn't keep one corner of his mouth from lifting. When she blinked and raised her gaze to his, he drank slowly of the dark brew. In the next moment she looked away and hurried to the other end of the counter. He continued to watch her, rewarded when every few seconds she'd glance over her shoulder at him with wary eyes.

He set his cup down. The drink paled by comparison to the pricey coffee served in the fancy shops, but Jim Palmer from the apartment building had assured Luke that this little coffee shop had its advantages. A hot little waitress, Jim had said. Luke wished he could thank Jim for his offhand comment.

"Told you she was a looker," Jim said.

Luke saw Jim also watched the flustered Pixie. He merely shrugged and traced the rim of his coffee cup with one finger, tamping down his excitement. At last he'd tracked down his prey after five days here in Indianapolis. Days of danger and confusion and desperation. Her beauty was a surprise. And the strength he felt in her promised a challenge.

"She be a pretty lass," Luke said.

Jim laughed, a hearty expression that matched the man's cheery nature and bright smile. "Maybe I should visit your Ireland, Luke, if you think she's only 'pretty.'"

Luke said nothing more as he watched the Pixie. She held magic. And he had only his duty to fight her—and the charm and cunning inherent to his clan. He would have to think on the best approach to gain his family's gold from the girl. Cornish Pixies had magic he'd only heard about, never seen. He wouldn't make a mistake now and send her back into hiding.

She'd responded to his small bit of charm, her skin flushed pink as her pupils dilated. Her breath grew reedy as she'd leaned slightly toward him. He'd known the instant her confusion changed to anger. She'd fight him if he mentioned the treasure now. There were too many mortals in the place, and he couldn't gauge the strength of the Pixie's magic.

He glanced around the coffee shop again. Lots of electric lights and windows. Her effect on his body was instant; he didn't dare tangle with her mind right now. It could be deadly.

Luke stood and placed some of this time's paper money on the counter. He thanked God again for bringing him to his prey at last. And now that he'd found her, he was confident his stay would end within a fortnight.

He and Jim left the coffee shop and walked toward the apartment building a few blocks away. She'd been this close to him all this time? It nearly killed him to walk away from her without the treasure. He shook his head and stifled a groan of frustration.

Jim fell easily into step beside Luke, taking the

position nearest the street. A simple push from Luke
made the man choose that side each time they ventured
out together. The carriages without horses—cars, Luke
now knew—still disturbed him. Their noises and smells
didn't endear the vehicles to him and he held himself
rigid as one began to bleat loudly to their left.

Luke shook off his unease and they walked for a
while, turning away from the main street and the heaviest
traffic. Over the past week Jim proved himself an able if
unwitting companion on Luke's quests through the
downtown nightlife in his search for the Pixie. He'd
eased Luke's way among the party-loving people of
Indianapolis, his American manners allowing Luke to
observe the crowds as he waited for his senses and the
amber to react to the Pixie's presence.

He was pleased to discover pubs were the same in
the here and now as back in Ireland in his time. And once
the people here heard his accent, they seemed to excuse
his old-fashioned mannerisms and odd ways of wording
things. With little effort he passed just beneath their
notice. Except for the mortal women. Their eyes burned
him through his modern clothes. He didn't forget the

incident with the woman in the clothing store. His charm
was under tight rein, but still affected the mortals in ways
he hadn't imagined.

"Where do you want to try our luck tonight?" Jim
asked.

Luke knew his friend hadn't found him out. No. He
still believed Luke's tale that he worked for himself, as a
"consultant." Luke prowled the city looking for the
thieving Pixie, night and day, and his unusual hours were
his own concern.

The hunt had been his only concern, for the days
since leaving home he'd focused solely on finding his
uncle's treasure. Now that he'd found the Pixie? He had
no need to patronize the saloons where more than one
mortal woman had attempted a seduction. His body still
ached from merely breathing in the Pixie's scent. Hot and
sweet, like her fine little body.

Luke shook his head. "I be keepin' to my rooms this
eve, Jim."

"Yeah?" Jim shrugged in his easygoing manner.
"Well, the girls will wonder where you are. They like
those big shoulders and the funny way you talk." He

grinned. "But I think I can keep them busy."

Luke couldn't help but smile. Jim worked at one of the local corporations, places of which Luke heard much and cared little. No doubt the man needed the release the ale and women could give him from his dull occupation. Jim liked to try his own charm on the ladies of this city, and his success surprised Luke at first. He soon realized the pubs might seem like those in Ireland, but even the primmest looking mortal women were apparently as generous with their favors as the most seasoned serving girl back home.

"Have at them, friend," Luke said.

He had interest in one woman at present. The Pixie.

Chapter 5

Brianna reached the snug home she'd rented and took her first easy breath since facing the Braunach that afternoon. The little house was close to downtown, in a neighborhood of older homes, but afforded Brianna and Violet privacy despite this proximity. Small and snug, furnished for warmth and function, it suited her and her sister. She'd need its comfort tonight.

She'd had no doubt they would find her; hadn't her grandmother warned her that more comes with the gold than she imagined? They sent such an able-bodied Braunach, though. So shrewd and forthright. So hot and handsome. His charm and beauty was nothing compared to the strength she sensed in him. She couldn't stifle a shiver at the memory.

She shifted the brown bag of doughnuts in her arms to one side and unlocked the door. "Bloody Hell."

"That you, Miss Wellbrook?" a voice called from the kitchen. "Is there a problem?"

Brianna shut the door and walked through the living room. She pushed open the swinging door of the kitchen, forcing a smile for the elderly woman who looked after

Violet while Brianna was at the coffee shop.

"No problem, Mrs. Henning." Brianna withdrew a bit of American money and placed it in Mrs. Henning's hand. "I'm just tired."

"No doubt." The plump woman clicked her tongue as she picked up her sturdy brown purse from the counter. "Toiling in that restaurant all day long."

Brianna's smile widened at the woman's staunch support. She'd only known Mrs. Henning for a short while and already she seemed to take both Brianna and Violet to her heart. Without a touch of glimmer, too.

True, Brianna would rather spend her time with Violet than serving folks at the coffee shop. The fortune tucked away would certainly allow her to go and do anything she wished. She wouldn't use the gold for her own comfort. That was certain.

"It's not that bad, really." Brianna held up the bag in her arm. The paper gave off its sweet greasy smell to fill the kitchen. "And they let me take the leftover treats home."

An answering smile curved the woman's mouth. "Violet's favorites." Her wrinkled brow furrowed. "Not that the sprite will eat much of anything tonight."

Brianna set the bag on the counter, her stomach twisting. "Is she all right?"

"Yes, yes. But she's so tired."

"Yes, the medicine has that effect." Brianna nodded, her throat tight. "Did she say her stomach hurts?"

Mrs. Henning gave a small nod and Brianna's own stomach clenched again. She patted Brianna's hand before donning her sweater. "I gave her the vitamins, Miss Wellbrook." She studied Brianna for a moment. "You remember to take care of yourself, too. The little one needs you."

The woman couldn't know how true her words were.

"Thank you again, Mrs. Henning," Brianna said. "Have a good night."

The lady clicked her tongue in sympathy and took her leave. Brianna sank down into the chair beside the little table in the center of the room. She knew she should check on Violet. She needed to collect herself before facing the child; she needed to center her strength. She looked down at her shaking hands and placed them flat on the tabletop, closing her eyes to slow her pulse, to calm her spirit. She was tired. That was true. Fatigue from her job was only one reason, however. The bloody Braunach had found her. Damn him to Hell!

As to the stolen Braunach gold, Brianna hid it well with a simple spell her mother had taught her years ago. She prayed it would withstand the Braunach's keen senses.

"Brianna?" Violet called from her bedroom.

The faint beloved voice dispelled Brianna's musings. "Yes, love."

She rose from the table and brushed her hands over her rumpled shirt and faded blue jeans. Her canvas sneakers making no sound, she made her way toward the little bedroom at the back of the house. Cheery yellow curtains dressed the one small window of the bedroom, a quilt in faded, lovely colors—wrought by the hands of some unknown woman and left here—covered the narrow wooden bed. And there, nestled among the quilt and sheets was the reason Brianna took what wasn't hers and came to this place. And she would do it again in a heartbeat.

Her little sister smiled. "You're home."

Brianna's heart ached to see the paleness of Violet's smooth cheeks, the dark smudges beneath those large blue eyes. She sat down on the bed and ran her fingers through the wispy golden hair on Violet's head. "And you should be sleeping, love."

Violet shook her head. She struggled as she sat up and leaned against the headboard. "I slept all afternoon, Brianna."

The mutinous set of her little mouth pleased Brianna and she couldn't help but smile.

"What about some soup for dinner, Violet?" she asked. "And a bit of television?"

The little girl clasped her hands, her face infused with a touch of color. "Oh, yes!"

Brianna laughed, her heart a bit lighter, and dropped a lingering kiss on her sister's brow. No fever there, she was relieved to note.

"I shall heat up some soup then, love." She stood and walked to the doorway. "And if you eat all of it I have a treat for you."

"Ben and Jerry's ice cream?" Violet asked.

Brianna smiled as she shook her head. Despite her

family's affinity for magic, nothing pleased her sister more than the frozen treat made by two round men in Vermont. Next to television, it was one of the few delights for the child here in America.

"Not tonight, I'm afraid," Brianna said. "But the doughnuts look very tasty."

Violet's mouth was a small O of delight. "Doughnuts? Yum!"

Brianna's spirits lifted as she went into the kitchen to ready her sister's dinner tray. After getting Violet settled on the plump couch in front of the television, she carefully measured out the medicine the child had to take for some weeks further. The tray at Violet's elbow held a steaming bowl of rich tomato soup and a plate with a precious chocolate doughnut, and after taking her medicine with a grimace the little girl set on her meal. Brianna watched her for a moment, making sure she ate and was comfortable, before escaping to her bedroom.

Brianna opened the closet door and knelt before it. She closed her eyes and murmured words taught to her by her mother when she was near Violet's age. A glow began at the back wall of the closet, heating her face as it grew brighter. As the warmth grew she opened her eyes and smiled, relief flooding her. Gold sparkled brightly before her. A king's ransom in stolen Braunach gold hidden in her closet, revealed to assure Brianna that Violet's treatments would continue. The gold's very presence that was so vital to Violet's health was dangerous to Brianna.

Brianna's sister suffered from a rare blood disorder, a sickness no Pixie magic had managed to cure. After much research she discovered this city with a strange name at the very edge of the key's power. Far less well-known than other cities such as London or New York, Indianapolis had seemed a fitting place in which to hide. Until now. It boasted a fine children's hospital, though getting the child such care would take a lot of money.

Two hundred years earlier one of their ancestors had stolen the gold from the MacDonald clan of Braunach. No Pixie had touched it since, and by legend it wasn't to be used except in a matter of life or death. Brianna stoically shook her head. This was surely such a matter.

Pixies avoided government constraints, like passports or customs officials. The less attention they drew, the better to avoid questions. And surely an abundance of gold coins would draw more than questions. So with the crystal key she leapt to America, risking the danger such a trip would pose to Violet for the promise of healing her for good.

To Brianna's eye she had more than enough gold for the little girl's remaining treatments. The city boasted many museums and antique shops where she traded the coins for American currency. The doctors and staff at the hospital, with the help of a bit of magic, believed not only that the child was Brianna's daughter but that a large trust was held for the child to pay for her treatments. To her relief Brianna wouldn't have to endure the prying an application for health insurance would entail, or the questions it would raise.

Brianna whispered a few more words and the glow before her faded. The room was cool now and, except for a slight shimmer on the back wall of the closet, the gold was concealed once more. After saying a prayer that evoked less magic and more Christianity, she rose and shut the closet door tight. *Please don't let the Braunach find the gold, Lord.*

She stripped off her simple work clothes and donned a thick soft robe. Reaching into the front pocket of the denim jeans she'd worn, she withdrew the small crystal key. Multi-faceted and pale blue in color, the key nestled in the palm of her hand. She found it amazing such a small piece of cut stone could affect such magic.

Carved from one piece of crystal from a deep cave on the Cornish coastline, the key had been in Brianna's family from time interminable though she'd never seen it before her grandmother told her the remarkable tale. Grandmother had warned Brianna to take care. That more came with the gold than she imagined. And more than magic came with the key itself. Of that, Brianna had serious doubts. For aside from getting her and her sister here to Indianapolis, the key had done nothing to keep the Braunach from her.

The MacDonald Braunach's gaze had heated her flesh, and she suspected it was due to more than the guilt she felt for snatching his family's gold. She believed he wasn't from this time. He seemed... odd and out of fashion despite wearing jeans and a simple flannel shirt. He was strong and handsome. That was true. And dangerous. Laughter reached her ears then, sweet and light. A smile curved her lips as thoughts of the MacDonald at last fled her mind.

She joined Violet in the living room and was pleased to see most of the little girl's soup, and all of the doughnut, was gone. The child laughed at a cartoon on the television and Brianna settled down beside her. She wrapped her arms around the girl's narrow shoulders and cuddled on the couch with her until the child's lids drooped over her beautiful eyes. When Violet's face was soft with sleep, a smile still lingering on her rosebud mouth, Brianna carried her sister to her bed once more.

***

Luke awoke in his large empty bed and stared at the plaster ceiling of the flat, planning his next move against the Pixie. He fingered the treasured amber tied around his neck as he let his mind work. She wouldn't give up the gold. Not willingly. Braunach were known for their charm, and Luke possessed his share in abundance. Hadn't more than one woman here fallen victim to it without his intention? True, he hadn't indulged with any of them. And honor was but one reason; none had

61

aroused the fire that filled him when he had glimpsed the lovely Pixie behind that counter.

She recognized him for what he was, he'd known. He'd read it in her look, her demeanor, as she trembled before him.

He rose and walked into the bathroom set close to his bed. Convenient this, he admitted as he saw to his morning duties in the raised, water-filled chamber pot. After a steaming shower, he wiped the mist off the mirror above the washstand and shaved off a day's growth of beard with a light throwaway shaver he'd found at a nearby store. He raked his fingers through his thick auburn locks and regarded himself in the mirror for a moment.

The Pixie was here, just as the Leprechaun O'Shey had told him. And she had the gold; of that Luke had no doubt. Her magic was far stronger than his charm and cunning, though. It would take a delicate hand to wrest the treasure from the girl, fragile though she appeared. Pixies weren't all lightness and beauty. He'd never seen one fairer, 'twas true. However, appearances were not to be believed where she was concerned.

He toweled off and dressed in the clothes he favored in this time: denim jeans topped with another soft shirt made of flannel. He pulled on a pair of thick white socks and padded into the living area of the flat.

The apartment wasn't any more attractive than when he first arrived. It was close to any number of markets where he could buy the sweet and crunchy cereal with the sea captain on the box, though. He poured a generous amount of the cereal into a large bowl, took chilled milk from the cold box and sat himself at the table. Not long after, a knock came at the door.

"Hey, Luke!"

He recognized Jim's voice. He glanced at the beige clock set high on one wall and frowned to see it was ten o'clock. Whyever was Jim here at this hour?

"Aye," Luke called.

He placed his empty bowl on the counter and opened the door. His friend stood there, dressed in knit pants gathered at his ankles and a gray pullover shirt. Sneakers, Luke had come to know, finished his friend's dress. Ah, he knew now. It was Saturday, the day the men in their building took full advantage of their free time to exercise or stroll the walks downtown looking for amusement. The weather was obliging, and Luke admitted spring was as good a time as any to be here and now.

"What's up, Luke?" Jim asked.

Luke resisted the urge to look skyward as he had when first hearing the odd greeting. He shrugged his shoulders. "Just finishing breaking my fast, Jim. What is… up with you?"

Jim grinned. "Thought we'd go jogging down by the White River."

The river whose name bore little resemblance to its condition, Luke mused. A bracing run would suit him and allow him time to consider his next move against the Pixie. "Aye."

While Jim waited, flipping through images on the television set in one corner of the living room with the small box in his hand, Luke went into the bedroom and changed into a blue sweatshirt and running pants. The city offered plenty of shops that sold these comfortable clothes, and they made up his wardrobe along with the jeans and flannel shirts. Ah the shoes, though. Luke loved these sneakers, and had bought more pairs than he could possibly use in the short time he expected to be here.

He laced up a pair of white sneakers trimmed in bright green, the ones Uncle Seamus would much love. Wincing at the thought, he left the bedroom and joined his friend. "Ready, then?"

Jim nodded and they left the apartment, bound for the wide brick walkways that snaked along the shore of the river.

Chapter 6

At the coffee shop, Brianna poured the grounds into the coffee maker. Her work didn't challenge her much, for which she was grateful. And she earned the money that kept her and Violet in food and shelter. She wouldn't use her magic for her own gain, any more than she would use the gold.

It was Saturday, and the coffee shop was as busy as any work day in the city. She deftly poured cups of coffee for the customers seated at the long counter. The patrons were primarily men, and she dodged smiles and veiled attempts at seduction as she went about her simple duties.

Another glance about the coffee shop showed her the Braunach wasn't here. In truth she didn't need her eyes to be sure; she would feel him if he came close to her again. No doubt he would be here soon, too. And she didn't need her Pixie senses to know that, either.

Ever since arriving at the shop that morning, an odd sensation had set her nerves to tingling. The crystal key vibrated deep within the front pocket of her jeans as well. Still no sign of the Braunach but they were a cunning clan, the MacDonalds. She wouldn't be surprised if he could watch her without her seeing him.

Thankfully, Violet had seemed stronger this morning. No doubt Mrs. Henning would have her able hands full with the little sprite. It was a pity the child would have to endure another treatment at the hospital on Monday. The poking and prodding hurt Brianna as much as her little sister. At least the hospital was bright and cheery, the staff friendly and caring.

The doctors assured Brianna that the treatment and medicines were working, although they were frustratingly slow. The doctors said the child's weak blood was growing stronger with each addition of an unknown savior's blood dripped into one thin arm. Brianna didn't understand all the technical terms the doctors used, but she now knew the child's illness well. Hemolytic Anemia, caused by an infection she'd contracted back home. Brianna prayed each day that the new blood and the medicine would heal the child. If not, Violet would have to endure a surgery that Brianna would rather not contemplate.

The little bell above the door tinkled yet again, and

with relief she noted the MacDonald didn't enter. Just a round little man with dark eyes. Brianna narrowed her gaze on him, finally letting out a breath as he sat himself at one of the tables lining the wall of windows that faced the street. Something about him seemed familiar, though she couldn't place him. Her breath grew short as he began to tap his stubby fingers on the tabletop.

"Hey, Bree."

Brianna jumped and turned to face Lori. "Oh!"

Lori placed a hand on Brianna's shoulder. "Jeez, Bree. What's wrong?"

Brianna glanced back at the dark little man but whatever odd sensation she had was silent now. "Nothing's wrong, Lori." She brushed back a strand of hair that had escaped her ponytail and offered the woman a smile. "I'm just tired."

"You need a day off," Lori said. "Boss man will let you."

Brianna shook her head. "I have my Sundays free. And Mr. Shepard gives me enough time off for Violet's treatments."

Lori clicked her tongue. "He doesn't mind, Bree.

You, me and the kids in the kitchen pretty much run this place and he likes it that way."

Mr. Shepard was another blessing in this place, his concern secured without the use of Pixie magic.

"I know," Brianna said. "But I can work the days she's well enough to stay with Mrs. Henning. I don't want to think about asking for more time."

"But what about you?" Lori asked.

"Me?" Brianna laughed without humor. "What about me? I'm well."

Lori straightened, her black curls bouncing as she nodded. "I saw that handsome devil eyeing you yesterday, Bree."

The Braunach. A devil? No, but just as dangerous. Brianna feigned confusion. "I don't know who you're talking about."

"Ha!" Lori laughed. "The one with the auburn curls and big green eyes, Bree. Ooh, and big shoulders. Long legs." She winked. "Don't tell me you didn't notice him."

Brianna opened her mouth to argue but the door's jingling bell cut off her words. A glance past Lori's shoulder told her that the "handsome devil" had returned at last. Bloody beautiful.

Lori followed her gaze, then turned to flash a cheeky grin in Brianna's direction. "Oh, and you didn't notice him? Although I have to say his blond friend isn't half bad, either."

Brianna hadn't noticed the blond man standing beside the Braunach; how could she, with the Braunach's moss green eyes fastened on her with an intensity that shook her? The key in her pocket began to vibrate softly, moving gently against her thigh. As she stood rooted to the floor in her lace-up sneakers, he approached.

His gait was easy and his shoulders rolled as he stalked her. The hanging lights caught the red in his thick hair, hair that was still damp. His plaid shirt stretched across his broad shoulders; his faded jeans hugged his powerful legs. She brought her gaze back to his face. The crooked smile she glimpsed there caused her mouth to tighten. The crystal key in her pocket shifted and she pressed her palm against the small bulge it made. *Strength, Brianna. Center your strength.*

"Good afternoon, lass," he drawled.

***

Luke drank in the unease he saw on the Pixie's lovely face. Her body trembled, and he more than suspected it wasn't fear causing her to shake. Nay, her blue eyes flashed at him, and he felt it straight to his belly.

He managed to keep from grinning as he and Jim sat at the counter. The girl turned from him and attempted to busy herself, but like yesterday her hands trembled. She was adept at her work, comfortable with the gadgets and workings of the shop. This told him she was from this time if not this place. Her moves were halting and jerky, showing her unease. He hid his grin of satisfaction. Good. She wasn't immune to his charm. She wouldn't be immune to his cunning, either.

"Great run this morning, Luke," Jim said. "And we have the rest of the day to… entertain ourselves."

Luke nodded, glancing up to find a tall dark-haired girl standing before him.

"Coffee?" she asked.

Her eyes held more promise than the hot brew. It was like this with most mortal women he'd met here. It seemed his charm slipped his control easily since his

71

time jump. Before he had cause to deflect her attentions, she turned to Jim and flashed him a bright smile.

"Coffee," Jim returned. He leaned on the counter. "And something sweet, I think. Any suggestions?"

The girl gave a throaty laugh and placed a hand on one shapely hip. "Anything you like."

Little was different in this time and place between the sexes, then. Jim had boasted over the past few days that the women here liked to "have a good time," as he put it.

"And what's your name?" he heard Jim ask the girl.

Luke soon dismissed their conversation and folded his hands on the counter. He watched the Pixie and as he stared at her round little bottom caressed by her jeans, he thought there could be worse things than waiting for her to face him again. He didn't have long to wait, however.

"Bree, see to Jim's friend, wouldja?" the dark-haired serving girl said.

Was that an English curse the Pixie muttered before letting out a sigh? He did smile then. She approached him, her hands in small fists at her sides.

"What can I get you?" she asked.

He arched a brow at her. "Coffee, lass." He inclined his head toward a plate of round treats he now knew were doughnuts. "And one of those sweets, pray."

She followed his gaze to the tray behind the counter and nodded. Turning from him again, she went to the tray and returned with a small plate holding the pastry. She placed it in front of him, the thick china slipping onto the counter with a clatter. He shot her an amused glance as he bit into the doughnut, and licked the chocolate icing off his lips. She spun on her heel and retrieved the coffee pot. He watched as she fill his coffee cup, thankful her nerves held long enough to keep from spilling it. Steam rose from the hot brew, and he didn't relish wearing it.

She faced him then, a look of something other than subservience on her face. "Will there be anything else?" she asked him.

"Aye, lass." He sobered his expression and leaned toward her. "And you know full well what it is I want."

That flash appeared again in her blue eyes, sending a spark through him. "You bloody—"

He smiled then, a grin he knew could charm the starch out of a potato. She blinked long lashes as she fell

73

silent, her rosy mouth agape.

"Easy, lass," he chuckled.

A string of colorful curses spilled from her rosebud mouth, too low to be heard clearly by anyone but himself. Shaking her head, she stomped to where the tall, dark-haired girl stood stacking coffee cups, untying the apron spanning her narrow waist as she went. "I need a bit of a break, Lori."

The other girl nodded and Luke could only watch as the Pixie escaped through the doors that must lead to the kitchen. Luke bounded off the stool, not caring about the speculative glances from both the waitress and Jim. He shot out the door and raced around the back of the coffee shop to prevent the Pixie's escape.

He found the girl in the alleyway behind the shop, her hands wrapped around her middle as she rocked against the brick wall at her back. She banged her fists against the wall then, all the while murmuring words he didn't recognize. Luke felt a blast of heat strike him as the Pixie's hair floated about her.

The next instant her eyes snapped open, focused intently on him. "Go away, Braunach!"

Caught in the thrall of her spell, he watched her skin glow, her eyes glimmer.

"You be havin' what I want, Pixie." Luke braced himself for another strike as he stepped closer, his heart racing as his breath grew short. "I shall have it."

She stepped back, stilling her hands. The heat in the air ceased as quickly as it had come forth but she didn't relax her rigid stance. She eyed him, her gaze sharp. "It's mine."

"You will give it to me, lass." He crossed his arms over his chest and glared down at her. "You will not win."

"I will, Braunach." She raised her pointy little chin and glared back up at him. "I have more power than you!"

Luke grabbed her by the arms, and a spark of a different kind coursed through him. His body shook with sensual awareness, her bare skin scorching his palms. He stared into her eyes, grown round in surprise. She gasped, her mouth a pink, moist target he couldn't deny. He sealed his lips to hers, tasting deeply of a sweetness more delicious than the chocolate doughnut. Sweeter than anything he'd ever tasted. She whimpered, then returned the kiss with an ardor that stunned him.

***

Brianna couldn't think with the Braunach's beguiling mouth weaving a magic she'd never before encountered. Hot and demanding, then slow and teasing, his lips and tongue thrilled her. His smell filled her senses, fresh and spicy. Her head echoed with the sound of her heartbeat as he deepened the kiss, and she closed her eyes.

He grabbed her to him, cradling her with his hands as he pressed her against the bricks at her back. The strength of him, the sheer size of his fit body, should have frightened her. And it did, though she feared for her sanity, not her safety. She wanted nothing more than to rub against his hard flesh as she gave in to the feelings he sent through her.

He brought his mouth to her ear, licking and nibbling as she collapsed against the wall. Her hands measured the breadth of his shoulders, the ridges in his back she could feel through his soft flannel shirt.

"Ah, lass," he purred, his mouth hot on her neck.

"My God, you are sweet."

After indulging in a few more moments of the Braunach's heady passion, Brianna took in a ragged breath and pushed him away. When she opened her eyes, she found him staring down at her in a combination of ardor and confusion. He was confused? Then what the bloody hell was she?

"Leave me," she whispered.

Was that her voice, husky and low? He shook his head and brought his mouth to hers once more. She evaded the kiss with a turn of her head and pressed herself fully against the wall at her back. At least her legs would have some time to learn how to hold her up again. He seemed to recover himself at last and he eased away from her. She managed to keep from whimpering as she lost contact with his body.

"I…" He raked his fingers through his auburn locks and let out a breath. "That was not…"

She crossed her arms, hiding her trembling hands as she affected an expression she hoped he would take as indifference. "No matter," she said. "You won't have the treasure, Braunach. Or me."

He blinked at her, his mouth dropping open. His brow furrowed. "I had not thought to take you, lass," he growled. "Not here, in this alleyway. Not now."

But she hadn't missed his arousal through his jeans, pressed against her in that moment when passion had ruled them both. Even now her belly clenched with a wanting she barely understood. "Leave me," she said again.

"Aye." He shook himself with a groan, at last giving a nod. "But know this, Pixie. This is not the end of it."

He stalked out of the alley, and she said a silent prayer of thanks. Oh, the Braunach was dangerous indeed. And to more than her hidden gold.

Chapter 7

"What's up with you, Luke?" Jim asked.

Luke lifted his gaze from his mug of ale and regarded Jim for a moment. A woman was draped over Jim, her eyes regarding Luke with open invitation despite that position. Luke just shook his head and drank deeply of the dark ale. Thankfully, Jim took little offense as he turned his attention to the girl with the too-bright blond hair. Another woman joined them, with inky black hair and eyes and a practiced pout on her full mouth. Luke had little trouble ignoring her lure despite her surface attractiveness.

Luke had learned that several pubs downtown brewed their own ale, a fact each employee proudly declared every time he and Jim patronized one of the places. Luke thought the places weren't much different than the taprooms back home, save for the pulsing music and odd modern clothes. He'd avoided the pubs since finding the Pixie's location, but tonight he found he needed the diversion. This pub was loud and crowded and the perfect place for Luke to lose himself for an hour or two.

He signaled the waiter for another ale and folded his hands on the dark wood table. The dark-haired girl leaned close enough for him to smell her cloying perfume.

"How's it hangin', handsome?" she asked, placing her hand on his thigh.

Hanging? He smiled and took her hand from him, putting as much distance between them as he could. She muttered something he couldn't make out but he wouldn't turn another smile on her. His charm was out of control tonight, and he had enough on his mind without having this forward woman on his hands.

He studied his hands then, recalling whom they'd held and touched and caressed just that afternoon.

He hadn't meant to kiss the Pixie. That was certain. When he'd found her in the alley, a swirl of magic about her, he had only briefly feared for his safety. The hunted, vulnerable look in her beautiful blue eyes had struck him, though he hadn't missed her strength. She drew him to her as easily as if she'd asked him to take her instead of demanding he leave her alone. He doubted he would've stopped had they been anywhere besides that dirty alleyway.

Ah God, she'd been sweet. And she'd fit him like no other. She'd given herself to him for those too-brief moments, and he hadn't needed her Pixie magic to know she'd felt it.

She'd touched him too, arched against his arousal until he'd thought he'd burst. Recalling her body, all supple and giving, made him harden now. She'd accused him of wanting to take her along with the treasure? Aye, he did want her. Wanted to peel the simple T-shirt and blue jeans from her body and know her like he suspected he'd never known another woman. He was honorable, damn his own hide, and there in Indianapolis for one reason: the gold needed to restore his uncle's sanity. He wouldn't let the saucy little Pixie sway him from that duty despite her assurances that he was the sole aggressor in that alley.

That dampened his lust. He downed his full mug of ale and stood. Leaning over, he moved the blond girl's fingers from Jim's shoulder and gave him a shake.

Jim disengaged himself from her and blinked up at Luke, a lazy smile curving one corner of his mouth. "Wwhat?" his eyes cleared. "Hey, Luke."

"I'm going home," Luke said. Jim began to rise but Luke shook his head. He glanced at the girl and ignored the hungry stare he got in return. "Don't get up," he said to Jim. "Good night."

Jim nodded. "Good night."

Ignoring the glances from the dark-haired girl and those he garnered from women during the short walk between their table and the door, Luke stepped out onto the sidewalk and made his way toward his flat. The spring evening was cool, and he welcomed the chill. He wouldn't think about the Pixie. The way she had felt in his arms, though. So soft and yielding... Muttering a curse, he continued on.

The next morning he awoke before daybreak, an odd tickling on his neck, his chest. He'd been dreaming about the Pixie, of their kiss in the alleyway. He'd done more than just kiss her in his dream too, and the erection pulsing against that small stroking hand told him his body remembered. A hand? He jerked awake, stunned to find a woman in his bed.

She grinned at him, flipping back a curtain of black

hair. "Hey there, handsome," she purred.

Ah God, the woman from the pub, the friend of Jim's partner. Luke sat up, holding the sheets over his middle. "What are you doing here?"

"Jim and Tandy gave me a ride home." She shrugged one shoulder, letting a shirt he now recognized as one of his flannels droop suggestively. "I didn't want to spoil their good time so he let me into your place with your key."

Luke thought for a moment, trying to make sense of her words as she flicked her tongue in his ear. His key? God, he'd given Jim a key when the man gave him his. Some sort of modern emergency plan, a "you watch my back, I'll watch yours," thing that Luke hadn't really understood.

He leaned away from her. "See here, lass—"

"Ooh, that accent," she said. She ran her hands over his chest, his belly. "And this body. Why don't we have a little fun?"

Despite his denial his body was still hard from his dream. He didn't want her, though. He couldn't imagine taking his pleasure in this seasoned woman. She stroked him through the sheet anyway, arousing him with her hand until he felt desire separate from her, from even himself. When she pulled the sheets from him, when she lowered her mouth to take him in it, he closed his eyes and leaned back on his elbows.

The amber was cold against his throat but the woman's mouth was hot, slick. Even the harlot in the dell hadn't possessed the skill of this one. With her soft lips on his flesh, her nipping teeth and swirling tongue driving everything from his mind, he indulged himself for several wild moments.

"Aye," he growled. His hips thrust upward as he clenched the sheets with both hands. "Aye…"

His blood rushed in his ears as he held on to his control. Before his climax took him, before he could spill his seed, she rose and held him tight with one hand.

"Do you want it?" she purred.

He stared into her eyes, his passion at its peak, his charm completely out of control. Aye he wanted it, wanted this. He wanted to throw his damnable honor out the thick-paned window and toss the wench on her back. Wanted to drive deep into her until she cried and begged for her own release. And he'd give it to her. He'd send her to the heavens while he let himself go at last.

"Nay," he rasped. He removed her hand and climbed out of bed, wrapping the sheet around his waist. "I… Go, then. Please."

She pouted, that expression that did nothing for him last night and diminished any lust he'd felt a moment ago.

"Jim said you don't take any women home from the pubs," she said. She stood, his shirt gaping open to show her naked body beneath. "But I felt it, Luke. You wanted me. You liked what I did to you."

Luke didn't want to hurt the girl but he had to get her out of here. He smiled and employed his Braunach charm to its fullest.

"Now, lass," he said, tilting his head to one side. "You don't want to lie with me."

She began to nod, then stared blankly at him. As she lost that predatory gleam he knew his charm was working. She touched her face, her neck, and took in shallow breaths. "Now you want to go home, lass." He picked up the small pile of her clothes at the floor near his bed and handed them to her. "You want to take your things and go to Jim's place."

She nodded. "Y-yes."

He urged her toward the door, pushing her gently backwards until she was out of his bedroom. She turned then and he knew the exact moment the spell was broken.

She spun to face him. "Hey, wait a minute!"

Luke opened the door and gently pushed her out into the hallway. "Jim's place, lass."

She blinked in confusion, then nodded again. She looked down at the clothes in her hands. "But, your shirt."

The shirt now carrying her perfume? He smiled and that unfocused look came into her eyes again. "Keep it."

He closed the door and leaned against it, holding the sheet with one hand. Raking his fingers through his hair, he set the woman from his mind as easily as he'd set her from his apartment. First came the dream, the most erotic images he'd ever encountered dancing through his mind as he took all the Pixie offered. Then he finds this mortal harlot in his bed? He'd nearly let her unman him.

He had to find the gold and get the hell out of

Indianapolis before his bloody MacDonald charm bit him in his sheet-covered backside.

***

Brianna set the medicine spoon down on the bedside table and brushed a lock of golden hair from Violet's cheek. "There, love."

The little girl settled down beneath the quilt and sighed. "I don't want to go, Brianna."

Though softly-spoken, she knew the child's protest was heart-felt. The treatments made Violet ill, and so tired she could scarcely leave her bed. Tomorrow would hopefully be one of her last visits, if the doctors' promises were to be believed. An examination could indeed prove that miracle. And the afternoon appointment would allow Brianna the opportunity this morning to sell a bit more of the blasted Braunach's gold.

The Braunach. He wanted the gold, that was obvious. Oh, his kiss! She wouldn't think about him. Or his lips. Or his hands. Or the way he'd felt as he pressed against her. She stifled a shiver.

"You have the whole of the morning to read or watch TV, Violet." Brianna straightened and crossed her arms. "Please don't drive poor Mrs. Henning mad."

Violet snuggled into her pillow and yawned. At last she nodded. Her eyes snapped open and she shot a glance at Brianna. "You'll be there, Brianna? Won't you be there?"

Brianna put on a bright smile and patted the little girl's hand. "Of course, love." She brought Violet's hand to her mouth and kissed it before setting it beside her on the quilt. "Aren't I always there with you?"

"Yes." She yawned again. "You're very good."

Brianna blinked. Violet's trust struck her like a living thing. "Good night, love."

She left her sister's room and closed the door quietly behind her. Oh, if she were only as good as her little sister presumed. Well, she would endeavor to be as good as her sister needed. To be the woman her family wanted her to be. To be as strong as she would have to be to face down the Braunach again and again until at last he surrendered any claim to the gold that was saving her sister's life. His bloody charm wouldn't make her lose control again. She would not be moved.

The whole of this day she'd kept to the snug little

house. Sunday marked a day of watching movies and making cookies. Violet seemed well today, aside from the paleness that still blanketed her smooth skin, the slightly swollen belly that showed beneath the pink sparkly sweater. Her eyes were clear, her smile bright. Now the evening was upon them, and Brianna had no other way to divert her mind from the MacDonald and the danger he represented to her sister's fragile recovery.

Brianna padded into her bedroom, ignoring for the moment the hidden treasure at the back of her closet. She stripped off her jeans and T-shirt, shrugged into her thick bathrobe and tucked the crystal key in the robe's pocket. She walked into the bathroom set in the hallway between her room and Violet's and hung her robe carefully on a hook on the back of the door. A hot shower would both soothe and refresh her. The tingling spray of water soon had her thinking of nothing more than the pleasure of it and the good night's sleep that would follow. She couldn't help but remember the Braunach's touch on her, as if he touched her bare skin. Her breasts tingled as she recalled his hard body pressed to her, rubbing against her. How could she face him down and protect her sister, if her body was so weak as to crave his touch even now?

She slumped against the cool tiles at her back and cried, her tears as hot as the shower spray.

She wouldn't be foolish enough to find herself alone with the man. That was certain. Her grandmother had warned her about their cunning. That was true. And their charm, though until today she hadn't given that trait more than a passing thought. She wouldn't think about his incredible kiss one moment longer. Tomorrow she would worry about the MacDonald. After she saw he sister through another treatment and safely settled in her little bed once more. Focusing on Violet's needs was all she needed to quiet her desire for the Braunach and his bloody beautiful mouth.

She finished her shower and was soon curled in her own bed, the key's satin ribbon wound around one wrist. Sleep found her with blessed ease and she welcomed it. She couldn't control her dreams, however, and as she slept, images of the Braunach filled her mind and the crystal key hummed softly in the darkened room.

Chapter 8

Luke stepped into the coffee shop Monday morning and quickly looked around the place.

"She isn't here."

He turned to find the tall, buxom waitress eyeing him with familiarity from behind the counter. Feigning ignorance, he smiled at her. "I am not lookin' for anyone."

The girl, Lori he remembered, laughed. "Bree's with her sister today."

Sister? His stomach clenched. There was more than one Pixie here in Indianapolis? He hid his apprehension at that particular disclosure. "I don't… Ah."

Lori placed a hand on her hip, a gesture he had often seen her make, and clicked her tongue. "You tore after her Saturday, handsome."

Luke's cheeks flushed hot at the girl's perception. Well, he wouldn't speak of it with this mortal. His weakness for the Pixie wasn't her concern. Nay, he would employ his clan's charm, and to great effect unless he missed his guess. Surely she wouldn't prove any more resistant than the doxie had been yesterday morning.

91

He glanced around the coffee shop again, nearly empty at this odd time between the nooning meal and dinner. Good. He folded his big frame and settled on the stool closest to the girl.

"You know much of the lass," he said. He fixed a crooked grin on her. "Tell me."

Lori blinked, her mouth falling open. She began to shake her head but Luke gave a soft laugh, one he knew to be full of promises a lass couldn't resist. The girl flushed, her trembling fingers running over her brow.

"Bree's with her sister…"

"Luke," he said.

She smiled, a heated expression, and her fingers slid down her cheek to her throat as she leaned her head back a bit. "Luke."

He folded his arms and placed them on the counter. "Tell me, Lori," he whispered.

Lori had to lean close to hear him, precisely what Luke had anticipated. He placed his hand over hers on the counter and the girl gave a gasp.

"I have need to speak with… Bree, Lori. That is all. I just want to speak with her."

A slow steady stroke to her fingers, innocent and not, had her breathing fast and shallow.

"Luke…"

His eyes bore into hers and he watched her pupils dilate. Her tongue flicked out to moisten her lips and Luke hid his satisfaction. Now the words would flow from her like warm honey.

"Where does she live, Lori?" he asked.

He gave her a slow perusal. Her breasts rose and fell rapidly. Smiling, he settled his gaze on her face once more.

"Pray, tell me where I can find her," he softly urged.

Lori looked around the coffee shop, no doubt torn between the lure he used and the loyalty to her friend. Admirable, that last. She opened her mouth and leaned closer still.

"Bree is—"

"Luke!"

Luke glanced up to see Jim enter. In that instant the charm was broken. Lori straightened and recovered herself. Running her fingers over her hair, she stepped away from the counter as Luke cursed inwardly.

He nodded in Jim's direction. "Jim."

Jim clapped him on the shoulder and settled himself beside him. "Escaped from the office early and thought I'd come and grab a cup." He smiled at Lori, who still looked flushed, before turning to Luke again. "I'm buyin'. I owe you for Saturday night."

Luke arched a brow in question.

"The minute you left the place, that girl was all over me." Jim jabbed his elbow in Luke's ribs. "I barely made it through the night. Had to get rid of her friend, though. Heard you left her hangin'."

Luke wouldn't admit to what he'd let the lass do to him before he recovered his control and his sanity at last.

"Sorry, friend," Luke said. "Don't give my key to any other lasses."

"Okay." Jim laughed. "Thought I was doing you a favor, is all."

Luke mustered a smile for Jim as he chatted about the coming week's work, his assignments. Yesterday had been Sunday, and Luke had left his flat after getting rid of the pub girl to attend mass at a downtown church. Saint Patrick's, he'd been pleased to note soon upon arriving in the city of now. After mass he'd stayed to pray for strength, for the duty given to him along with the amber pendant. Despite the amber growing warm in response, he knew prayer alone wouldn't save Uncle Seamus. The Pixie held the answer to his uncle's health and sanity in her strong, delicate hands. Where was she hiding?

He glanced up at Lori, now fully recovered and apparently ignorant of his attempt to charm the information out of her as she flirted with Jim. He would have his answers. He would find the Pixie and her sister. He cursed again. Two Pixies? How the bloody hell would he fight two of them?

He drank his coffee and pondered his next step. There was nothing else for it. He would have to follow the Pixie and track her to her den. Then he would use every ounce of charm the good Lord had blessed him with to wrest the treasure from her.

***

"Brianna."

Brianna stirred in the hard plastic chair set close to the bed and rubbed the sleep from her eyes. She blinked as she glanced around the sterile room, the smell of it stinging her nostrils. The room was both odd and familiar; a place like this should never be familiar, especially to a child.

Violet lay in the bed, a tube filled with healing blood snaking down to flow into one slender arm. Her hospital gown looked huge on her, the faded sprigged cotton a drab color that went well with the rest of the treatment room. Brianna touched Violet's free arm. It looked so fragile, the veins outlined beneath the pearly skin. She stroked the pale skin, wishing she could warm it with her fingers.

"I'm here, love," Brianna said.

The child winced as she shifted in the bed. Her face was still ghostly white, even against the pristine hospital sheets. "I miss Mama."

Brianna bit her tongue to keep from echoing Violet's sentiment. Their mother had been as kind as she was beautiful, a talented Pixie who lavished both magic and love on her two daughters. So many years separated Brianna and Violet's birth, their mother always said that she had the best of both worlds with one sprite to raise and another to befriend. She was gone these past three years, closely following their father's death. She took Violet's chilled hand in her own. "I know, love."

"And I miss Grandmother," Violet said. "I want to go home."

"You're not well enough to go home, Violet," Brianna said. "You know that."

"I know." Violet's lower lip trembled but she raised her little chin in an expression Brianna recognized as Pixie pride. "But I shall get better, Brianna."

A genuine smile curved Brianna's lips. "Yes, you shall. And then I'll take you home to Grandmother."

Muffled sounds could be heard in the hallway outside the thick wooden door: wheels on gurneys, shuffling feet, hushed voices. The door suddenly opened with a soft whooshing sound. Brianna turned to find Violet's doctor entering the room.

"Mrs. Wellbrook?" he asked.

Relief struck Brianna. His mode of address told her the glimmering charm was still working; he believed her to be Violet's mother.

"Hello, Dr. Noble," she said.

He nodded to her and picked up the folder sitting on the small metal table beside the bed. The papers rustled as he perused the mountain of information it undoubtedly possessed on her little sister's condition by now.

"Hmm," he said, at last setting the folder down once again. He touched the bag of blood and its tube, checking for something Brianna couldn't fathom. Then he smiled winningly in the child's direction. "Hello, Violet. Feeling any better today?"

Violet nodded, a cheeky grin for the handsome doctor on her little face. What a flirt. Brianna smiled inwardly.

"I feel much better, Dr. Noble," Violet said.

Brianna blinked at that. With competent hands, Dr. Noble pushed up the folds of Violet's sprigged hospital gown and rubbed her swollen belly. Violet didn't hold her grin during the examination, a fact that told Brianna much more than she would like.

"Hmm," he said again. He gently lowered the child's gown and turned to Brianna. "Mrs. Wellbrook, may I speak with you?"

Brianna's stomach clenched sickeningly at his

request. "Y-yes." She handed Violet a well-worn book from the stack set in a basket beneath the metal table. "I'll just be a moment, love."

Violet nodded and took the book she'd read too many times already. Dr. Noble held the door for Brianna and she preceded him into the hallway. He let the door rock closed as she turned to face him.

"Tell me," she said.

"I'm not as pleased with Violet's progress as I could be, Mrs. Wellbrook," the doctor said. "Is she taking her Prednisone?"

"Yes," Brianna said. "She balks, but I make certain she gets each measured dose."

Dr. Noble nodded, brushing his fingers through his fair hair. "She has no fever," he allowed. "But her spleen has not returned to its normal size as yet."

Brianna's heart began to pound. "Please, doctor." She took a breath and straightened her spine. "Please tell me all of it."

After a brief hesitation he nodded. "If the swelling doesn't go down soon…" Regret filled his blue eyes. "We'll have to remove her spleen."

Though she'd known of this possibility all along, she couldn't bear the thought of anyone taking a knife to Violet's creamy skin. "What... what else can be done?"

"We've discussed this, Mrs. Wellbrook. Violet's body is producing healthy red blood cells. The infection she contracted some time ago left her spleen inflamed. It's destroying the blood cells faster than she can make them."

"What of the blood transfusions?" Brianna asked. "They're helping, aren't they?"

Dr. Noble nodded. "But if the steroid she's taking doesn't begin to work, Violet will need surgery."

It all crashed in on her at once. Too late, her mind whispered. All for nothing. Taking the gold, facing the MacDonald. All for nothing.

Brianna hugged her middle and trembled, lost in her misery for a selfish moment. Not far down the hall, a stack of files fell to the floor, scattering papers everywhere. She reined in her fear, her power, and looked at the mess she'd caused. Several nurses bent to pick up the papers, puzzlement on their faces. She straightened and faced Dr. Noble. "I pray it won't come to that, Doctor."

"This surgery's done quite often," Dr. Noble said. "My main concern would be Violet's frailty."

Violet was a frail little thing now. Oh, if only the doctor could have seen her sister before the illness that left her in such dire straits. Bright and bubbly, troublesome and wonderful. And now Violet was a mere ghost of her former self.

"What do we do for the time-being?" she asked.

"I'll see her again next week," he said. "Perhaps her body will rally and respond more readily to the steroid. Just make certain she rests and takes her iron as well."

Yes, iron. The vitamins Mrs. Henning and she dutifully administered each morning.

"I will," she said.

Dr. Noble smiled at her. "Then I'll go say good-bye to Violet."

Brianna gave him a moment alone with her sister, using the time to gather her own strength. *Oh, please let her get well,* she prayed. If anything were to happen to Violet now… She wouldn't think about it. Or about the Braunach, damn him. He couldn't know the power he held in his skillful hands. He had the power to take Violet's slight chance of the survival along with his family's gold.

Chapter 9

Luke walked up Meridian Street, the busy thoroughfare that bisected the city. Tall buildings bracketed both sides of the street, and he was pleased to keep to the sidewalk beside the ones to his right. Along the wide street, horseless coaches—cars, he mentally corrected himself—roared and bleated as they made their way. Initially surprised to find horse-drawn cabs sharing the space with the loud vehicles, Luke now thought the poor harnessed animals appeared more dispirited than not as their clumsy drivers plodded them along the crowded streets. Pity there was no room for the animals to trot.

The day was bright, though the chill of winter still clung to the breeze that ruffled his hair. Men dressed for a busy workday, in short jackets and long thin neck cloths, hurried to their jobs on the walk, all ignoring him in his casual flannel shirt, thick white undershirt and jeans. Yes, the men ignored him; not so with the women.

Young and old, women wearing skirts and men's pants and harried young mothers pushing babies in prams, the females of this time openly perused his fine form. Breathy greetings and chirpy hellos met his ears, and he idly nodded in return. His charm was out of his control this day, so focused was he on his prey. He did nothing to rein it in; he would do nothing to take advantage of its effect either. He was dimly aware of a few of the more brazen women following in his wake, their perfume and giggles reaching him.

Putting the city women out of his mind, he fingered the amber pendant at the base of his throat. It was cold beneath the undershirt. He cursed under his breath. Three days had passed since he'd laid eyes on the Pixie. Three days during which he'd made no progress in reclaiming the gold. There had been no sign of her at the coffee shop since Saturday, and he was loathe to try his charm on the waitress Lori again. With his thoughts in such a jumble, he didn't trust his power. And the last thing he needed was another forward female offering him something he didn't want or need. His shame with the woman from the pub still tore at him.

Two Pixies. Amazing. He knew the Cornish Pixies to value family, as much as his own clan did. He hoped only one sister accompanied the Pixie Lori called Bree. Bree. It was an odd name, one that didn't seem to fit the lass. Nay, it was too hard a sound for so delicate a beauty. He laughed out loud. She was delicate, aye. And possessed a will so strong he was still no closer to recovering the gold and restoring his uncle's mind than when he time jumped nearly a fortnight ago.

As it had too often over the past three days, his mind went back to their kiss in the alleyway. Magic and passion had swirled around them, a heady mix that warmed him now. Aye, his body heated to think about her sweet lips, her yielding form. Both her vulnerability and her anger had been clear. He didn't need her face before him to recall the blue fire in those beautiful eyes. He wouldn't give in to the temptation. He would keep his wits about him. And his heart secured. The thought of emotion stilled him.

"Troublesome lass," he muttered.

He heard a laugh then, low and sly and just to his right. He shot a glance down the nearest alleyway, his heart pounding. He saw a shuffling shape there in the shadows, or so he thought. Then nothing but a few large trash cans. Again he fingered the amber, but it was cold as ice against his throat.

Luke raked his fingers through his hair and looked up and down the street. Ignoring the feminine smiles thrown in his direction, he entered the nearest coffee house and ordered a tall something or other with cream. He handed his money to the skinny bespectacled man behind the counter and took the warm paper cup.

After settling down at a too-small table, he removed the cup's plastic lid and blew at the fragrant steam snaking up from the drink. He took a sip, swiping at the foam left on his upper lip, and frowned into the cup. Ah, who did he think was he fooling? He didn't want the fancy coffee any more than he wanted the mortal women here in Indianapolis. He wanted the Pixie. And he would find her today.

He tossed the still-full cup into the nearest can and left, turning toward the little coffee shop. Two blocks off the busy Meridian Street, the shop was a welcome sight to him. He wouldn't ponder the reason now, wouldn't think of the pretty package of magic who might right at this moment stand behind the counter. Nay. The *gold* was vital. His heart and body did not matter in this. And if tangling with the Pixie was necessary, he'd do his best.

106

Finally he smiled, anticipating the challenge "Bree" represented.

One step into the coffee shop brought her into his sights. The tension left his body in a rush, and he rolled his shoulders in response. In that moment she turned, her eyes large and questioning and soft. Then she blinked, inky black lashes that shielded her gaze just long enough for her guard to return. He felt it, like a wall between them. Now her stance was falsely dismissive as she gazed at him with indifference. He grinned. He hadn't missed it; that awareness was real. And he would use it today to bring her under his lure. To wrap his mind around hers as he longed to with their bodies.

***

Brianna braced herself for the MacDonald's power as her body flushed with response. Oh, she knew he didn't possess true magic; her senses would have picked up on it that first day. She wouldn't think about the kiss that had woven a different kind of spell. He was bloody handsome with that grin on his face, his green eyes twinkling. One rake of that green gaze over her showed his interest. She wouldn't tell herself that he cared for her. No. He'd use his power to steal away the gold, to snatch from Violet the only chance she had at recovery.

"The handsome devil has you in his sights, Bree," Lori said. The laughing tone in Lori's voice turned soft. "Thank God."

Brianna glanced at her but found her friend smiling and talking with a customer farther down the counter. She slid her gaze once more to the Braunach, grudgingly admiring the easy way he moved as he approached her and sat down at the counter. She took note of his dress, the soft flannel shirt that spanned his shoulders open to reveal a thick woven shirt of white beneath. At his neck she saw a glimpse of leather or rawhide, a thin strip that drew her eyes to his strong throat. Then up to his finely-chiseled features, his lovely mouth. Oh his eyes... A deep green, sparkling with untold mirth and pleasure. Mmm.

Brianna blinked and gave herself a shake. What the devil ailed her?

"'Mornin', lass," he said.

The voice, smooth as honey, poured over her. Once more, she straightened. "Good morning, sir."

He folded his arms and leaned on the counter. "Coffee, lass." He grinned and her heart tripped a beat. "If you will."

Brianna's mouth fell open but no words came forth. He arched one reddish eyebrow.

"Hmm?" Her fingers itched to trace that brow, to touch his tanned skin. To dip her fingertip into the tiny cleft in that strong chin. "Oh!" She shook herself again. "C-coffee."

He gave a slow nod. Taking a breath, she turned from him and lifted the full pot of just-brewed coffee. She placed a thick china cup before him and managed to fill it without spilling a drop. She watched as he lifted it to his mouth, blowing slightly to cool it before taking a sip. His tongue slid out to lick his lips and she thought back to that kiss in the alleyway behind the coffee shop. That mouth, that tongue, had spun its own magic around her. He set the cup back down and regarded her for a long moment, his eyes telling her he too recalled that kiss. Sighing, she relaxed and studied the green fire burning in those eyes.

"Mmm." He licked his lips again. "Just what I

109

needed."

Brianna's skin grew hotter. He ran those beautiful eyes over her and her stomach tightened, her breasts tingled. Aware of only him, she gazed openly at his fit body before settling on his face once more.

He smiled then, slow and deliberate, and that brought her back to herself. She gave a jerk and spilled coffee over her hand. "Ouch! Bloody hell!"

In a flash he took the pot from her and held her injured hand in his. At his touch she forgot the sting, forgot everything but his rough fingertips stroking over the back of her hand.

"It's just a little pink, lass," he soothed. Before she could stop him he lifted her hand to his mouth and dropped a gentle kiss on her injured flesh. "No need to fret."

She nodded, caught by his lure once more. "Th-thank you."

The MacDonald tugged her close and the sounds of the shop faded from her notice as he pinned her with his gaze. "I have need to speak with you… Bree."

Brianna nodded, her breathing shallow. "Y-yes."

"You have what I want."

Heat once more infused her and she gasped. She licked her lips and nodded, her throat thick.

"Take me to it, lass," he said.

She started to nod her agreement. Suddenly Violet's image floated before her, weak and wan and with eyes so full of trust she shuddered in response. The moment's thought gave her strength to pull away. "No!"

"Come, lass." His eyes still on her, he quirked a crooked grin at her. "Give over to me."

In that instant she recognized the morning's events for what it was: MacDonald charm. Close with the Braunach, his hand touching hers, was too intimate, too calculated. Anger filled her in a rush.

She jerked her hand from his and took two steps back from the counter. And she had almost fallen into his snare! "Go to the devil, MacDonald!"

At last he lost that smugness. Scowling, he crossed his arms over his chest. "You will yield, lass."

She opened her mouth to blister his ears when she realized their situation. Talk in the coffee shop had stilled and more than one pair of eyes was fastened on their confrontation. After a moment, the other patrons soon went back to their meals and conversations. Glaring at him, she placed her hands on her hips. "You won't have it, you Irish devil."

A soft chuckle came from him and her body twitched despite her mind's intentions. She wouldn't think about his throaty whisper in the alley, his firm lips, his strong arms holding her so tenderly. She wouldn't think of anything but Violet!

"Leave me," she whispered.

That green fire sparkled in his eyes and she was nearly lost again. "Now, lass," he teased. "Is that any way to treat a paying customer?"

Another step away from the counter brought her a touch of relief from his pull. "Don't think to use that bloody MacDonald charm on me."

He lost his grin at that and clenched his hands in fists, no doubt to keep from grabbing her to him. "If you would but listen—"

Brianna whirled away from him and hid in the kitchen. One of the kitchen workers, more boy than man, eyed her with mild concern and she waved away his interest. He went back to assembling and wrapping sandwiches and she closed her eyes.

Her strength returned slowly, her mind losing the fuzziness he'd put there. Oh, she wouldn't go into the alleyway. That was certain. She wouldn't dare risk his following her and using a far more potent charm than the one she'd just deflected. His lips, his hands… Her hands shook and she fisted them. Maybe her power wasn't as strong as she'd thought.

***

Luke watched the swinging door until it stilled, knowing the Pixie hid just inside the kitchen. He grunted with frustration. He'd almost had it all, her surrender and the gold. She wasn't immune to his charm, he allowed as he sipped his coffee. She was strong, through. Any other lass would've given him his answers. And their body, if he'd so desired.

He could still see her there, flushed and beautiful. Her breath coming fast through parted pink lips, her full breasts pressing against the thin shirt she wore. He grunted again, shifting in an effort to gain a bit of room in his jeans. Physical pleasures had no place in his quest.

By the saints, she was a sight. Hot and ripe and fashioned to specifications he hadn't even known he'd wanted.

The waitress, Lori, came over to him. She frowned at him as if she knew full well what he'd tried to do with the Pixie. With a flick of his head, he nodded toward the small puddle on the counter.

"The lass spilled a bit of coffee."

She clicked her tongue and wiped up the spill with a towel. "Bree's upset." She clenched the towel and glared at him. "Tell me that was an accident."

Luke feigned innocence as he had before with her, but he didn't dare employ his skills. Not now. "The coffee?"

Lori snorted. "Look, handsome. I don't know what your deal is, but I know guys like you. You zero in on a girl and use her to get what you want."

He couldn't argue with that, though she obviously believed he wanted something of a more carnal nature from the Pixie. "Aye."

Concern filled the girl's eyes and he once more knew the Pixie had woven her own magic on this mortal. "Bree has a lot on her plate."

He glanced at the stack of dishes behind the counter and shrugged again. Odd expression, that. "All right," he offered.

Lori blew out a sigh and leaned closer. "I'm watching you, handsome. Bree's not as strong as I am."

The girl couldn't have been more wrong, in his considered opinion. The Pixie was the strongest woman he had yet to encounter in this time or his. He stood and left the coffee shop, his mind formulating the next step in wearing down the lovely lass. Much as he disliked the notion, he would have to think like Daniel O'Shey. He would have to skulk in the shadows and track her to her den. A memory niggled, something he had glimpsed in the alley that morning. Something dank and cool, slithering among the shadows.

Shaking his head, he dismissed the thought and focused on the coming afternoon. And the distasteful task ahead.

***

"Go home, Bree," Lori said.

Brianna knew she should listen to Lori. She couldn't fiddle with the dishes and cups any longer. The shop wasn't open for dinner except on Fridays, which added to its allure as her temporary occupation. And the lunchtime crowd, even the latecomers, were long gone. Tea time was nonexistent here, and she really had nothing to keep her any longer.

Oh, she didn't delay going home to Violet. The bloody MacDonald was at the root of her unease. That odd sensation he'd left behind was stronger than ever this evening. Time and again she had looked up from her work, fully expecting the vexing man to be there in all his charm and glory. Hiding like a coward, she'd delayed the walk home. No one had ever accosted her; the safety of the neighborhood combined with a protection spell assured that.

"All right." Brianna removed her apron and hung it on one of the hooks right beside the kitchen door. "No doubt Mrs. Henning needs a bit of relief."

"Is your sister any better?" Lori asked.

Brianna opened her mouth to respond, surprised at herself. She never spoke of Violet to anyone, except to arrange her days off. And Mr. Shepard never questioned her requests, a marvel as she didn't use a shadow of glimmer in this place.

"The doctor…" She breathed in sharply. "The doctor says she might need surgery."

"Oh, no!"

Brianna waved her hand in the air, wishing she could ease her own worries so easily. "It's not definite. The doctor… he's worried she's still too frail."

Lori stepped closer and placed a hand on Brianna's shoulder. "You'll get her through it, Bree. You're strong."

Brianna looked at Lori in surprise, wishing she could be reassured by the words. Her eyes stung and she nodded. "Thank you." She took her cardigan sweater down from another hook and shrugged into it. "Good night, then."

Lori smiled. "Good night."

Brianna nodded and left the coffee shop, praying she were as strong as those around her seemed to believe.

Chapter 10

Luke's senses sharpened as the door of the coffee shop opened. From his vantage point a few storefronts down the street, he had watched for what seemed the whole afternoon. The bench was hard beneath him and the tension of the afternoon left him primed for the girl's appearance. The night was chilly, though his thick undershirt and flannel was all he needed.

The Pixie exited the shop, a thin pink sweater the only protection he could see. He quickly amended that assumption when he saw an ill-kempt man turn in her direction. He stood to follow the pair, but before the interloper could get within ten feet of her he jerked abruptly and walked away. Luke smiled and shook his head, his heart ceasing its pounding as quickly as it had begun. Of course the girl would employ a protection spell. No matter. If her spell drew a circle around her as she made her way on the street, he would simply wait until she was safely in her den before approaching her.

Moving soundlessly in his fine sneakers, he trailed her a short distance before she entered a neighborhood of small but finely-crafted houses. Quite different from both

the city and his own dull flat, the neighborhood appealed
to him. The tall trees brought the MacDonald dell to his
mind; the bright streetlamps shining through the spring
leaves cast dappled shadows on the street. Little wonder
the Pixie had chosen this location for her lair.

She stilled before a snug gray house set back from
the street. As if sensing something amiss, she turned in
his direction. Luke was too fast for her though, and the
stout old tree beside him provided fitting cover. He heard
her light footfalls once more and peeked around to see
her cross the front porch and enter the little house.

He waited, surprised when a round old woman soon
bustled out the front door and climbed into a car the
shape of a beetle bug. With a sound akin to bubbles
popping, the woman drove up the street and away from
the Pixie's den. He wouldn't waste a thought on the old
woman's identity. Now the Pixie was at his particular
brand of mercy. Her and her sister both.

Luke crept nearer to the house, his stomach churning
as he kept to the shadows. He had learned from Uncle
Seamus that a man must deal with all matters plainly, and
this stealth didn't sit well with him. This was different,

however. And surely his uncle would understand a bit of subterfuge used for the greater good. The Pixie had their gold, and she must be made to relinquish it; from his dealings with her up until now, she wouldn't give it up easily.

He raised up from his haunches to look through the lace-dressed window. The girl moved with grace about the house, and as he watched she emerged from what must be the kitchen with a tray holding food and drink. She set the tray on a low table before a threadbare couch, and straightened. Her hands at the small of her back, she stretched out the tension surely caused by her day rather than the light load she'd brought from the kitchen. She covered her mouth as she yawned, and exited the room down a narrow hallway.

A doubt niggled at him as he awaited her return: why did she toil in the coffee shop if she had the MacDonald gold? The house was far from luxurious. The furnishings were worn and the decorations simple. What had driven her to take what was theirs?

He set that thought aside and rose, intent on getting the answer to that question. She bore a different burden when she came to the couch once more. A tiny child, he was amazed to see. With tender care, the Pixie placed the wee one on the couch and covered her with a colorful woven blanket before switching on the television. Luke studied the child, who to his eyes had all the looks of a Pixie. Shining golden hair, thinner than the older girl's, and large eyes of the same remarkable blue set in a little heart-shaped face. No doubt this was the sister the waitress, Lori, had spoken of that day in the coffee shop.

The little Pixie was so small. So wan and pale. The one he sought, Bree, fussed about the child, giving her an elixir of some type and placing her hand on her forehead. A frown marred the perfection of her face, and Luke's heart clenched in his chest. The child was ill, and quite important to the Pixie caring for her so tenderly. He felt for her: hadn't his uncle's illness drive him across time and space?

"There, love," he heard the Pixie say to the little one.

The child smiled, a small expression that lit the room. "Thank you, Brianna."

Luke pulled back. Brianna? Ah, the name suited the lovely Pixie. He pulled his gaze from the two on the couch. He saw no sign of the gold, but the amber at his neck throbbed with a beat his pulse echoed. It was here. In this house. In her hands. Her magic was strong, and his encounters with her thus far confirmed that fact. She could easily hide the gold from anyone's notice, and he had none save his cunning and charm to win it from her. And after his attempt this afternoon, he had less faith in his own abilities than he liked.

She had kept herself from him, her body and her mind. She'd shown moments of weakness, and though the idea was distasteful he would exploit whatever advantage he had. His uncle hadn't raised a fool. He would find a way to best her, and on his own terms.

Luke stood, backing away from the window. He wouldn't confront the girl, not at present. The wee one needed her, and he wouldn't interfere tonight. He walked away from the house, knowing he would have little trouble finding it at a more opportune time. The amber eased its disquiet as he headed downtown, and his mind turned toward what he learned this evening.

The Pixie—Brianna, he thought again—and her sister had come here from Cornwall. Why, though? What circumstance drove her to take his family's gold, his uncle's only hope? They seemed comfortable with this time's trappings. He'd seen her work the money machine at the coffee shop enough to guess that they weren't from his time. His mind in a muddle, he went into his apartment and resigned himself to a less than restful night's sleep.

***

Brianna made her way to the coffee shop the next morning, fatigue dragging her down. Violet had been particularly pained last night, and had called for her often. This morning Brianna had dressed and readied for work despite her fatigue, and when Mrs. Henning came she left the child to the woman's care. Lord, she was tired. And she would work the dinner shift this evening to earn the money lost on days she stayed home with Violet.

"Brianna."

Brianna stiffened at the sound of the MacDonald's voice. When had he learned her name? She set that vexing thought aside and stared at him for a moment.

He stood beside the coffee shop, and how she'd

approached him without noticing was beyond her. The crystal key in her pocket gave a twitch, and she belatedly acknowledged it had been doing so for nearly a block.

"I don't have time for this, MacDonald," she said.

The man's brows drew together for a moment before that befuddling grin spread across his handsome face. "'Tis a beautiful mornin', lass. Surely you have time to discuss something important to both of us."

Brianna took in a breath, her hands in fists at her side. "I won't discuss this with you!"

His auburn locks ruffled in the gust of wind she created, but he stood his ground. "I'm not without powers, Pixie." He stepped closer and she felt that dangerous pull of him once more. "And you are not without vulnerabilities."

She blinked and Violet's face once more floated before her mind. Did the MacDonald know of her sister? Would he harm her? "Are you threatening me?"

Despite the peril he presented to herself, she didn't believe he would harm a child. Nothing in her sensed that kind of malevolence. Last night, after she'd gotten Violet tucked snuggly into bed, that odd prickling sensation had struck again. Shifting shadows at the window had given up nothing of their origin, and she'd dismissed the feeling as a result of the fatigue that still clung to her this morning.

"Ah, 'tis not a threat, Brianna." His grin widened and he stepped closer. "'Tis a promise on my honor."

"Your honor?" She snorted at that. "You come to claim the only chance—"

She snapped her mouth shut on the truth and the MacDonald stepped closer.

"What is this?" he asked.

He raised his hands to her arms but she danced out of his reach. She hurried into the coffee shop, confident that he wouldn't question her about the gold in front of a shop full of mortals.

"Good morning, Bree," Lori said.

With no more than a nod in Lori's direction, Brianna donned her apron and busied herself refilling coffee cups set before the patrons seated at the counter. The bell above the door tinkled, but she didn't need to look up to know the MacDonald entered. Bloody hell!

Despite her attempts at ignoring the man, her gaze

was drawn to him again and again. He sat at the counter for hours, doing nothing but sipping coffee and nibbling a sandwich. And watching her with that confounding green gaze.

***

Luke didn't hide his smile. Nothing demanded his attention this day, save for keeping an eye on the Pixie. And a more pleasant task he couldn't imagine. She was indeed vulnerable to him, as demonstrated in the flush of her cheek, the catch of her breath, whenever she stepped closer to his end of the counter. Far easier on his bottom than the bench proved last evening, he was content to bide his time on the cushioned stool. Lori served him, more cups of coffee than he could count, and he kept his vigil.

The Pixie had nearly told him all of it, in her anger if not under his lure. He wouldn't think of the tiny child, so ill and obviously dear to her. Perhaps the trip had proven too much for her fragile body.

The Pixie shot him a particularly flinty stare and he felt the tingle to his bones. Not unpleasant though, as the amber pendant warmed steadily against his throat with every step that brought her closer to him. His body responded in a manner that was becoming the norm when dealing with her. He didn't refrain from studying her delectable little body as she fairly trembled in ire, and he grew fully aroused. Well, he didn't dare leave the coffee shop now. Anyone would glimpse through his jeans the effect she had on him.

"Give it up, handsome."

Luke dismissed Lori's words with a wave of one hand. "Keep to your own concerns, lass."

She glared down at him. "Bree's concerns are her own."

Luke merely shook his head, refusing to raise his pique to match hers. "Why do you—?"

"Lori, please," Brianna said.

The waitress blinked and stared at the Pixie. She glanced at Luke as if daring him to accost her friend, finally stepping away. Luke regarded the Pixie with interest as she braced her hands on the counter and leaned toward him. His body hummed as her scent reached him, fresh and sweet. He sucked in a breath and studied her. Her eyes drew him, blue and sparkling, into their depths. His gaze fell to her mouth... He could picture his mouth on hers, her mouth on his body. She smiled, a wanton expression, and he jerked back. "You... you're trying to charm me?"

She muttered under her breath and straightened, breaking her spell as she tucked one strand of gold hair behind her ear. "I don't know what you're talking about, MacDonald."

Luke's passionate haze cleared, replaced swiftly by vexation. "I will win in this, lass."

"So you've said." She attempted an air of dismissal he didn't believe for a moment. "But you haven't won yet."

Luke grinned, a predatory expression that he knew she read for what it was. "The battle isn't over."

He stood and left the coffee shop. Tonight he would once more visit the snug little house. Aye, he would have his answers. And his gold.

***

Luke found himself outside the Pixie's house, though this time it was well past sunset. A benefit to sitting and watching for hours on end at the coffee shop was information. Although his prey never went more than few minutes before eyeing him, as patrons came in for the nooning meal she soon became too preoccupied to give him more than passing notice. And when her friend, Lori, expressed her unease that an obviously-tired Brianna would work late this evening, Luke had begun to form his plan. It was vastly easier to keep an eye on a the house in darkness; he had little care to arouse the suspicions of the Pixies' neighbors. He had been correct, though his plan hadn't progressed as he might have wished.

He had hoped to enter the house and search for the gold; he had little doubt his charm could keep the child occupied. The old woman he had seen the previous afternoon was within. He'd heard her as she spoke to the child, cajoling her to take her medicine or chiding her to keep to the couch and rest. And he was forced to bide his time, leaning against a tree placed conveniently beside the window at the side of the house. At least he felt comfortable there, as if he sat in the dell back in Ireland. Odd, though when he was near Brianna he felt that same comfort.

Now the little mite was alone in the drawing room, and Luke couldn't take his eyes from her. She was small and weak, yet he sensed her power was nearly as strong as her sister's. Whenever the old woman wasn't about, the child flipped through the television pictures without the device he thought was so clever. Books floated to her waiting hands from shelves set on the other side of the room. And her smile, though fleeting, caused his own lips to curve as she laughed at something she saw or read.

He settled back to wait for the old woman's dismissal upon Brianna's return. It was time enough for action. He fairly rubbed his hands together at the prospect.

The Pixie Brianna was strong, of which he had ample evidence. Their encounter this morning told him much of her powers. Her fatigue had made her vulnerable, if not to his charm than to his cunning. When she had attempted to charm him herself there in the coffee shop, he had felt a pull stronger than any he had yet encountered. His body still hummed with the awareness of that pull. She was a sensual being, a fact he couldn't ignore. The thought of that sweet body pressed to his, that hot mouth opening to him, had him thinking of a challenge of another kind. One which would yield both of them a treasure he dared not crave.

Letting out a curse, he settled against the stout tree, letting its rough bark serve to bring him back to himself. It was going to be a long night.

***

Brianna dragged her feet as she made her way home. Mr. Shepard had asked her to work the occasional dinner shift, and after allowing her to spend so many work days with Violet, she could not refuse on this particular Friday evening. At least the MacDonald had taken himself from her sight as the dinner crowd began to fill the shop. Her senses, though dull from fatigue, tingled as she neared the house. A shuffling behind her caused her pulse to race and she spun to find the source of the furtive sound. A dark shape, rounded and odd, moved between two trees across the street. In a moment there was nothing more; no sound or movement met her senses.

Dismissing her unease as fatigue, she chose to focus on Violet. She entered the house and closed the door snugly behind her. "I'm home, Mrs. Henning."

The little woman bustled out of the kitchen, a tired smile on her face. "Good evening, Miss." Her brown eyes crinkled with concern. "I don't mind staying late of an evening, dear. You look done in."

Brianna gave a weary sigh. "I'll survive, I wager."

She settled on the couch and flicked off the television. Belatedly, she realized she did the trick without the remote device.

"Odd, that," Mrs. Henning observed. "It's been doing that all day. Drove me mad, but the little sprite just laughed."

Brianna started. Oh, she would have to speak to Violet about using her magic so haphazardly. Cautious hope filled her at the prospect; this was the first evidence of the child using her talents since the time jump. She slanted a look at Mrs. Henning. "Maybe the television is broken," she offered.

The older woman simply shrugged and donned her coat. "I'll see you in the morning then, Miss."

Brianna murmured in response, her head settling on the back of the couch as the woman let herself out the door. She was so tired. She used her magic to turn off all

132

but one lamp and closed her eyes, taking a moment to gather her strength.

No sound came from Violet's bedroom as she tiptoed toward the little chamber. There her sister slept, as sweet as an angel and twice as pretty. She was still pale, but her cheeks were rosy from sleep and gave her the appearance of the child she had been in Cornwall. Before she'd gotten so very sick and driven Brianna to take such a drastic step. Perhaps the doctor was wrong. Perhaps Violet would get better and not need the drastic surgery.

Brianna stroked the silken hair and dropped a kiss on her sister's brow. Violet smiled in her sleep and snuggled into the fat pillow.

"Sleep well, love," Brianna whispered.

No response came from Violet and with each even breath the child took, Brianna at last felt the tension and fatigue of the day dissipate. She left the child's room, closing the door tight and returning to the living room. Suddenly the crystal key in her pocket began to vibrate, and she froze. She glanced up, stunned to find a large figure looming in the center of the darkened room.

"Good evenin', lass."

Chapter 11

Luke relished the expression of surprise on the Pixie's face, evident despite the dimness of the room. Intrigued though not surprised, he watched it change into a scowl of intense displeasure.

"What the bloody hell are you doing here, MacDonald?" she rasped.

Her question was a hiss in the dark, but Luke kept his own reaction in check. Too long he had rested against the tree outside the window, and he was spoiling for a confrontation that seemed centuries in coming—two, to be precise. He would have to tread carefully. "What kind of greeting is that, Brianna?"

Her eyes narrowed as she stepped closer. She shot a glance down the hallway—he guessed the little one rested in one of the chambers down that hall—and faced him again. "You will leave my home, MacDonald."

Luke stepped closer to her. "Nay."

The Pixie shook with her ire, her hair swirling about her as her eyes flashed blue fire. His nape prickled and his skin felt hot, but he held his ground.

"You will not take the gold," she said.

He arched a brow at her. "You admit you have it, then?"

The girl shook and the floor seemed to vibrate beneath his feet. "Bloody hell!" Books flew off the shelves, one missing his shoulder by a hairsbreadth. "I need that gold, MacDonald."

"For what, pray?"

Her eyes widened and he saw it, the vulnerability he had glimpsed but a few times since finding her. Before she could react, he reached out and grabbed her arms. "Tell me, lass. Why did you take my gold?"

She fought him, shaking her head from side to side as the lone electric light in the room flickered. He held her close, praying he could ignore the lure of her as her curves touched every part of him.

"I can't!" she cried. "I can't—"

He cupped the back of her head, effectively ceasing her thrashing and bringing his gaze into direct contact with those incredible blue eyes. She blinked long lashes in confusion. He took her brief silence for the opportunity it represented. He stroked her nape, gentling her. "Tell me, Brianna."

The anger waned; he felt as much as saw it in the easing of her body. Unable to resist, he bent closer to her. He felt her heart beating against his chest, breathed in the intoxicating scent of her. Passion flared in her eyes, as powerful as the anger had filled them moments earlier.

"I… don't understand," she whispered.

He brushed her lips with his and gazed down at her.

"Passion, lass," he rasped. "I feel it, too."

Her lips moved, but no coherent sound came forth. Luke wouldn't wait any longer for a protest he doubted would come. He took her mouth, and their kiss exceeded his recollections of their encounter in the alleyway. She wound her arms around his neck and gave herself up to Luke and he was lost. He deepened the kiss and she purred in response, arching her body against his as she matched his urgency.

He nuzzled her ear, her throat. Her skin was soft and sweet and hot against his lips.

"MacDonald…"

"Luke," he said, his voice harsh in his ears.

She sighed. "Luke."

When she said his name he reacted, body and soul.

He shrugged out of his flannel shirt, letting it drop to the floor somewhere behind him. Her sweater was a hindrance he wouldn't endure another moment. He took it from her and stroked her back through the thin T-shirt before settling his palms on her round bottom and pulling her close. He hardened against her soft belly and pressed tighter still.

Her hands tugged on his undershirt, setting his skin aflame as they danced over his belly, his chest. Never before had such desire ruled him, and a voice in his head warned him to take care.

Luke turned and placed her on the couch, silently praying for control. Her breath coming fast, she leaned back on her elbows and watched him as he pulled his undershirt up and over his head. Her gaze was hot on him and his flesh tingled, though the response was quite different from when anger shimmered between them. She licked her lips and he let out a growl.

"I want you, Brianna," he said.

***

Brianna couldn't take her eyes from him. He was the most beautiful man she'd ever seen. She took in the broad shoulders, the strong chest covered with whirls of reddish hair that trailed down over his flat belly to the waistband of his jeans. The leather strip around his neck held a round slice of amber. The smooth stone gave off a soft glow in the darkened room. The light pulsed and she felt each beat in her heart. The key in her pocket trembled and she struggled to keep her wits about her.

"MacDonald…"

He grinned at her and its impact struck her very center. "Luke."

She smiled as he corrected her again. Luke. The name suited him, strong and pure. Desire for him hummed in her veins, a passion she saw reflected in his green gaze. She raised her arms to him. "Luke," she whispered.

He covered her, his body supported by his arms as he brought that beautiful mouth to hers once more. She whimpered with pleasure as he kissed her, her fingers twining through his thick hair. Her T-shirt a memory, his hands burned as he stroked her belly, her breasts, through her thin camisole. Her nipples tightened as his strong fingers stroked and fondled her through the lace.

Their jeans rasped against each other, the friction driving her mad. She'd never felt anything like what Luke made her feel with each movement of his big body against hers. She was pure though, despite the desires filling her addled mind as he dropped kisses on her throat. This was wrong, her conscience chided her. His passionate caresses, his murmurs of encouragement, the clean crisp smell of him… Oh, her mind was a muddle with him so ardently pressing upon her every sense! "Luke, please."

"Aye, lass."

He brought his mouth to her breast, sucking her nipple through the satin and lace. She arched, the sensation nearly her undoing. Just a moment longer, she told herself. Just a bit of satisfaction to ease the burning in her veins she suspected only he could appease.

Suddenly he stilled, raising his head to gaze down at her as his breathing rasped in the silent room. She wouldn't have to put him off, she saw. He shook his head with regret even as he eased away from her.

"We mustn't, Brianna." He kissed her mouth and brought his forehead to hers. "I know this as well."

Brianna couldn't resist running her hands over his shoulders even as she nodded agreement. He was so beautiful, his soul so pure she could see it shining through his eyes.

"Easy, lass." He gave her a crooked grin. "If you keep touching me, I may forget my honor."

She let her arms fall to the couch, at remarkable ease with the man she had believed her enemy these past days. "Your honor."

His brow furrowed. "Do you doubt a MacDonald, Pixie?"

She shook her head and brought a hand to his cheek. "No."

He dropped a kiss on her brow and eased her to a sitting position beside him. "Tell me, then."

She cuddled against him, taking in a deep breath. She couldn't ignore his strength, his support, and nodded her head. She had taken his gold, and her own honor demanded she offer an explanation for her actions. "It's my sister, Luke."

He stroked her hair and she took comfort from the action. "The little one."

Glancing at him, she saw only compassion on his features. She nodded again. "Violet." She took a breath. "She's ill."

"Aye." He grew quiet for a moment. "But… the gold. Why did you take it?"

Brianna couldn't face him as she told him all of it. He deserved the truth, though. And she wouldn't shrink from the task. She studied her hands, folded in her lap to keep from taking the strength he offered.

"She got sick in Cornwall, Luke. Months ago. We thought she was better, but then she grew so weak, so pale. The treatments were so expensive."

"So you… stole my gold?"

She faced him then, urging him to see what was so clear to her despite its dishonesty. "I didn't. One of my ancestors did, nearly two hundred years ago. I took it and came here, though. Wouldn't you do the same for someone you loved?"

He didn't say anything for a moment, though his gaze grew troubled. "Aye."

That one word urged her to at last share the burden that had been hers alone these long months. He covered her hands with one of his and she grabbed on for the solace she'd been without since leaving her family in Cornwall.

"I took the gold, Luke. I can't replace the treasure, I know. My sister needed care and the treatments are expensive." She took in a breath and let the tears come at last. "But she's not getting well fast enough. The doctor says…"

Luke held her, letting her cry all over his chest as he stroked her back. She sensed no lust now. Just compassion and caring and she held on to him.

"Easy, lass," he said. "Easy."

After a while Brianna sniffled and sat, wiping at her eyes. "If Violet doesn't get better, the doctor will have to perform surgery."

"Surgery?"

"He'll have to remove her spleen—one of her organs."

Luke sucked in a breath. "Nay."

She nodded, using the edge of her camisole to mop her cheeks. "Yes. Though he says she may still be too frail."

"She's a wee thing, Brianna."

"You won't take the gold back, Luke?" Brianna knelt on the couch and faced him fully. "Not now?"

***

Luke studied the Pixie, tenderness wrapping around his heart. He wanted her—aye, he would have to be a dead man to ignore the enticing picture she made there on the couch, all soft and rosy and rumpled. She was so strong, so determined to save the little one entrusted to her care. And the child needed the gold as much as his uncle did. He couldn't forcibly take away the little mite's chance at life, could he?

"I'll not take the treasure, lass. Not now."

She sagged with relief, wrapping her arms around his neck and kissing him soundly. Pulling back, she braced one hand on his chest. "Oh, this isn't because of what we nearly…?" Her eyes shone with fresh tears. "Have I traded my body now?"

"Never, Brianna." He grabbed her arms and held her away from him. "'Tis true, I want you. Like I've never wanted another woman. I'll not ease my body with an innocent, no matter the lure."

144

She blushed to the roots of her shining hair and lowered her lashes. "How did you know?"

"I felt it, lass," he said. "Your purity wrapped in all that passion."

She smiled, then sobered her expression. "But the gold. You want it back, and yet—"

"It is mine." Her expression grew guarded but before she could pull away he cupped her cheek. "And if I could think of another way to see the child well, I would reclaim my gold."

She stood then, wrapping her arms around her middle as she gave him her back. "You will go then." Resignation filled her voice despite the command. "There is nothing here for you."

He turned her and took her in his arms. "What I feel for you, lass. There is that. And it's so much more than desire. Don't you feel it?"

She studied him, looking for what, he wouldn't hazard a guess. "Yes."

He hugged her to him. "I need the gold, Brianna."

She stiffened, and he stroked her hair, her back.

"Back in my time, in my home, my uncle's mind is

145

not… well," Luke said. "The gold will restore his wits, I believe."

She pulled back and placed her hand on his cheek, the gesture comforting and nearly causing his knees to buckle. "Then you know full well what I've been through, Luke."

"Aye." He kissed her palm and placed it on his chest. "I shall find a way to see your sister well and my uncle's mind restored, lass."

She fingered the amber at his neck, and it throbbed in response. "This is your magic, Luke." Her brow furrowed, then her face filled with hope.

"Aye. 'Tis what brought me from my time to yours."

Her eyes sparkled with hope. "Oh, you can time jump and find a simple cure for Violet's illness!"

He shook his head. "Nay. I wish that were so. 'Tis not my amber but my uncle's. And save for tracking you, it has little power here for me."

Her shoulders sagged.

"But I shall find a way, Brianna," he said. "You have my word."

She smiled then, an expression as beautiful as he had

yet seen. "On your honor."

He chuckled. "Aye."

Suddenly he couldn't leave her, not with their blossoming feelings swirling about them as surely as the magic she spun so easily. She'd snagged his heart, he feared. He had given her his word, and on more matters than the gold.

"I don't want you to leave," she said.

She seemed surprised by her own words, though he didn't press her for their meaning. He pulled on his thick undershirt, watching as she gracefully donned her simple T-shirt and smoothed her golden locks. Lord, she was lovely. Dare he hope she could one day belong to him?

"I was going to eat a little something and go to bed." Her mouth was an O of surprise. "That is… to sleep."

He laughed at her unease, sharing the feeling himself. "Ah. What of the soup the sprite ate for dinner, lass?"

"You…?" She smiled knowingly. "You watched over her."

"I waited for you, Brianna." Luke shrugged. "Forever, it seems."

His own words stunned him. Thankfully, she took nothing more from his statement.

"Two hundred years, at least," she smiled. "I shall heat some soup, then. And yesterday I brought home some bread from the coffee shop."

She took herself into the little kitchen adjacent to the drawing room and he settled on the couch once more. Day-old bread when she had the MacDonald gold at her fingertips? He knew the truth then. The gold was for the child. Brianna was noble. And his match. He'd had a true glimpse of the purity of her spirit. And her passion.

He would have to find a way to see both the child and his uncle well, and that was no small task. Perhaps he was indeed blessed with his uncle's own luck. He fingered the still-warm amber pendant. Hadn't it brought Brianna into his life?

Chapter 12

Brianna hummed to herself as she worked behind the counter, her mind on all that had changed since yesterday. The MacDonald—Luke, she smiled to herself—stayed long after their modest meal was over, sharing his own fears for his uncle that mirrored hers for Violet. They kissed some more, delicious kisses that woke yearnings within her for so much more, and cuddled on the couch together. The tenderness they shared was only one reason for her mood this morning; after keeping her burden to herself all these weeks, her heart was fairly floating.

"You look happy, Bree."

She smiled in Lori's direction, shrugging her shoulders even as she continued to hum. "It's a lovely morning, is all."

Her friend eyed her closely. Lori opened her mouth, no doubt to question her further, but stilled as the bell jingled above the door. Brianna turned and caught Luke's eye as he entered the shop. A pleasant tingle coursed through her, the crystal key thrumming in her pocket as her heart beat in rhythm.

149

"So that's it!" Lori said.

Brianna glanced at Lori to find her wearing a knowing grin. Her cheeks heated but she said nothing. Instead she faced Luke and smiled.

He returned the expression, his green eyes sparkling. "Good mornin', lass."

His smooth deep voice brought to mind the sweet words he had whispered in her ear last night. She was seized with the urge to fly over the counter and wrap her arms around his neck. Restraining herself, she wiped her damp palms on her thighs and stood her ground. "Good morning, Luke."

As he approached the counter, she saw his blond friend followed on his heels. That man too must have sensed something, for he threw her a puzzled glance before settling beside Luke.

"Coffee, please," the man said.

Brianna looked at Luke. He nodded his agreement and she hurried to fill their cups. She set the pot back on the burner and turned to the counter.

Luke caught her wrist and gently tugged her closer to him. "How are you this mornin', Brianna?"

That sounded quite intimate! She checked to see if his friend had heard his question, but the man seemed taken with Lori as those two traded flirts and banter.

"I'm fine, Luke," Brianna said.

He sipped his coffee, regarding her over the rim of his cup. She gazed into his eyes, feeling the pull that no longer frightened her. At least not as it had when she feared for her safety rather than her virtue. She took a step back nonetheless, still overwhelmed by his charm.

***

Luke watched Brianna as she distanced herself from him, if only by an arm's length. From the very moment he'd entered the shop he'd wanted to touch her, to hold her like he had last night. Now she removed herself. Taking a breath, he turned the conversation to a safer if no less vital topic. "Is the little mite well?"

Brianna nodded. "She's better today. And…" She stepped close again and lowered her voice to a whisper. "And she has been using her magic."

Luke barked out a laugh, causing the other patrons to look their way. He leaned one elbow on the counter, and grinned. "I saw her flip through the pictures on the television and retrieve books from the shelves."

She smiled at that. "Oh, but she's driving poor Mrs. Henning mad."

Her sparkling gaze told him the truth of it. "You don't seem upset, lass."

She nodded with enthusiasm. "I admit I'm encouraged."

Luke took her hand and gently stroked the back of it. Only someone who knew of the Faery folk would understand the import of her words. "She's getting better, Brianna." Brianna's eyes shone with the sheen of tears, and he longed to carry her burden for her. "Lass…"

"She has another treatment at the hospital in a few days," she said.

"Do you want me to come with you?" he asked. "That is, if the wee one agrees."

"Oh, that isn't…" Her guard was still up then, but she nodded in the next moment. "Yes. Thank you, Luke."

He glanced over at Jim, then leaned closer. "May I take you to dinner this evenin', Brianna?"

"I can't. You're… you're welcome to come to my house."

He felt it again, the pull toward her that had nothing to do with MacDonald gold. Her eyes showed that she, too, remembered all that had happened—and nearly happened—in her little house. He was honorable, and she knew that. Her virtue would be safe. He shook his head. Even if it killed him, she would remain pure. He was in no position to make an offer fitting to her granting him that gift. Was he actually considering marriage?

He swallowed. "I shall bring dinner, then. Have you had pizza?"

Lori and Jim both shot him an look of confusion at that question, and Brianna hid her smile. "Of course. It's a favorite of Violet's, too."

"Good." He stared into the empty coffee cup for a moment before bringing his gaze to hers. "Do you think she'll like me?"

Brianna smiled. "Why, MacDonald! You told me you were not without power. Surely a tiny child doesn't frighten you?"

Luke shook his head, laughing deep in his throat. "I daresay the thought of spending time with the two of you does much to make me doubt my powers, Brianna."

She nodded again and went back to her work, fairly bouncing on the balls of her feet as she served the other patrons. Lori refilled his coffee cup, giving him a look of warning along with the brew, and left him to his thoughts as he drank.

All night he had puzzled over it. However would he satisfy his family and Brianna's? He would have to return home and speak to his uncle soon. He'd made a promise to Brianna, one he prayed he could keep with his uncle's help. He could only hope the man's mind hadn't deteriorated much further in his absence.

***

"Is he handsome, Brianna?" Violet asked.

Brianna turned from the front window and looked at her sister. The child was in high spirits this evening and Mrs. Henning reported that she'd hardly complained about a sore belly all day. Brianna prayed this meant the child was healing, but she would await judgment until Dr. Noble looked at her on Monday.

"Yes, love," Brianna said. "The Braunach is handsome." Violet's eyes twinkled and Brianna laughed. "Now you will behave yourself."

Violet's eyes rounded in a look of innocence that didn't fool Brianna for a moment. "I was just asking." Violet fiddled with her pretty pink sweater, still too large for her. "He's bringing pizza?"

Brianna smiled. "Yes, Violet. And he—"

A knock on the front door gave her a start. She peered out the window and saw Luke standing there, two flat boxes held easily in one arm. He grinned at her and her heart gave a flip. Oh, she would have to be very careful.

She opened the door and he strode inside.

"Dinner is served!" he said.

Violet giggled, her eyes riveted to the man. Luke bowed in the child's direction, his smile replaced by a solemn expression.

"Is this the Pixie Violet?" he asked.

Violet popped off the couch. She executed a perfect curtsey and batted her eyes at him. "Hello, MacDonald."

"Luke, sprite." Luke grinned. "If you please."

Violet nodded and looked at Brianna. "Oh you were right, Brianna. He's most handsome."

Brianna's cheeks heated as Luke arched a brow at

155

her. Instead of attempting an argument she couldn't possibly make, she went into the kitchen for plates and napkins. Bracing her hands on the table, she closed her eyes. She could hear Violet talking in the next room, her chatter interrupted now and again by Luke's deep voice. There was something so comfortable about the situation, yet she couldn't hope it would last. Luke had promised to find a way to get Violet well, and she sensed his spirit was as true as his word. But what of the gold? And his uncle? How could she expect him to come to her aid when his family was depending on his success two hundred years away?

"Brianna?" Luke asked.

She whirled to face him, grabbing up the dishes and napkins from the table. "Here... here are the plates."

He stepped in and took the small stack from her, his brow furrowed. "What's wrong?"

She shook her head. "I'm a bit tired, is all."

The quirk of his lips told her he didn't believe her, but he said nothing more of it. With a flick of his head, he directed her into the living room. "The sprite is hungry, lass. As am I."

Brianna nodded and left the kitchen, Luke trailing behind her.

***

Luke knew the Pixie had much to worry about: her sister, the gold, his promise. He didn't need her magic to sense her unease. After leaving the coffee shop that afternoon, he hadn't been able to find any solution save for returning to Ireland.

The child was as fascinating as her sister, and he could see clearly now she needed the gold as much as his uncle did. Pale despite the sparkle in her eyes, Violet would no doubt fail without the treatments Brianna's determination found and his gold financed.

"Brianna says you want to come to the hospital with us?" Violet asked.

Luke faced the sprite and smiled. Red sauce smeared her little mouth, and her cheeks bulged with pizza.

"Aye, Violet," he said. "I trust that's all right with you?"

"Oh, yes." She swallowed her bite of pizza. "You can keep Brianna company while I rest."

That told him much. The treatments must tire out the

mite, and at the sight of Brianna's knit brow he knew they took as much out of her.

"And maybe when you feel well I can take the two of you out and about?" he asked.

"Luke, that isn't—" Brianna began.

"Oh, yes!" Violet cried.

Luke laughed aloud then. "There are canals behind my flat, and they let out little boats to paddle. Would you like that?"

The child nodded with enthusiasm and even Brianna's eyes brightened at the prospect.

"A boat ride would be lovely," Brianna said.

"Aye." He lifted another slice of pizza and chuckled. "Though the waterway hardly compares to what we're used to, lass."

Brianna laughed, a musical sound that made his heart clench pleasantly. "I admit I miss the Cornish coast."

There it was, the difference spoken loud and clear. She was English; he as Irish as the clovers which dressed Uncle Seamus's finest shoes. She was Pixie and he was Braunach. Such unions were not forbidden, though.

"You have yet to see the ocean from Ireland's perspective, lass," he said. "Or from my time."

Brianna's blue eyes sparkled, a sight as lovely as the ocean itself on a summer morning. To wake to their beauty each day was something Luke had never imagined wanting so much. Ah, he did.

"I would love to see Ireland, Luke!" Violet said. "Your Ireland."

Luke smiled at the child. "I shall feel honored to show it to you, sprite."

Brianna's brow knit, and he knew her sister's illness as well as his easily-spoken promise weighed on her. She doubted him, despite her words of last evening to the contrary.

"Have you had enough to eat, Violet?" she asked the child.

At Violet's nod she rose and went into the kitchen, emerging with that bottle of medicine Luke had seen her give Violet before. The child pulled a face but Brianna cajoled her to take it, the blasted medicine that wasn't doing enough to heal Violet or give Luke back his gold.

Luke set the thought aside, preferring to let Brianna

lead the rest of the evening. The unspoken challenge of his other promise, to his uncle and family, hung in the air between them despite passing the time watching television and talking.

Violet yawned loudly not much more than an hour later.

"You must go to bed, love," Brianna said.

The child's pout was adorable and, though it charmed Luke, her sister was not so easily swayed.

"Oh, all right," Violet sighed. She shot a cheeky grin in Luke's direction. "It was lovely meeting you, Luke."

Luke stood and bowed to her once more. "The pleasure was mine, sprite." He looked over at Brianna, and took another step toward attachment. "Perhaps tomorrow we can have an outing?"

It was unfair to put the Pixie on the spot, he knew. He hid his smile as she obviously pondered the wisdom of it.

"Oh, yes!" Violet chirped.

"That…" Brianna gave a reluctant nod. "That would be lovely."

He won that challenge, he thought with some relief.

While Brianna settled her sister in her chamber, he cleared the mess of pizza boxes and plates and napkins into the kitchen. Standing in the middle of the modest room smaller than even in his cottage back home, he acknowledged again that the Pixie only used the gold for the child. More's the pity, for if a mercenary bone lurked in her delectable body he wouldn't hesitate to wrest the gold from her. As for now, he would bide his time and see if there was indeed a way to satisfy her family and his family. And his heart.

Chapter 13

"We're not there yet, are we Brianna?" Violet asked.

Violet seemed to shrink beside her, taking up less than half of her seat on the bus.

"Just a few more minutes, love," Brianna soothed.

She looked over at Luke, whose green eyes studied the child with worry. He gripped the handrail in front of him tightly, weathering the speed and sway of the vehicle as it made its noisy way uptown. He was an amazing man, and his speedy adjustment to the present time was but one reason she felt that way.

Yesterday he had done much to occupy Violet's mind—and her own, were she honest with herself. A ride in a horse-drawn hansom cab through downtown Indianapolis followed by dinner in a sidewalk café let all three of them focus on something other than sickness or doctors. The hours had passed with no talk of Violet's treatments or Luke's gold. Even she knew they couldn't put off that last topic for long.

"I'm eager to see this hospital of yours, Violet," Luke said.

Violet perked up at the sound of Luke's voice. "Oh,

it's nice enough. And Dr. Noble is nearly as handsome as you."

Luke grinned. "Is that so?"

Brianna met his gaze, and she knew he wanted her opinion of the doctor.

"And competent as well, pray?" he asked. "Surely he's a paragon."

The teasing tone was there but their relationship was so new, so as-yet-undefined, she guessed he wondered if another held her heart. She nearly laughed at that notion. No one before Luke had ever come close to her heart let alone her passion.

"Oh, there it is," Violet said.

Violet's voice, flat of emotion, broke through to both Brianna and Luke. The bus squealed to a halt and they rocked in their seats.

"Come, love." She forced a smile of encouragement and gave the child a squeeze. "Dr. Noble is waiting."

Luke lifted the child, causing her giggles to fill the bus and draw reluctant smiles from the other riders.

"Mustn't keep the man waiting, sprite," he said.

Violet clung to Luke's neck, a big smile on her pale

face. She was already happily under his thrall. If only Brianna could be so open about her own attraction to Luke. Giving herself a mental shake, she stood and followed the two of them off the bus.

***

The child weighed next to nothing in Luke's arms, and her trusting embrace caused his heart to swell. The little Pixie did nothing half-measure. And her hug told him she accepted him in the role in which he cast himself over the past two days. What the role entailed in whole, he wasn't quite so sure. Nevertheless, he would protect her as fiercely as her sister would.

Brianna was at alternate times both open and shuttered, her gaze worried and affectionate now. He knew she was attracted to him; even last evening, after the child went to bed, they had once more kissed and cuddled and tempted the honor that burned between them as strongly as the passion. He was confident he had her desire. But her trust? He suspected that was a treasure as precious as his family's gold.

After he saw Brianna followed, he crossed through the large glass doors that slid open at his first step in front of them. His nose wrinkled as an odd smell struck him, a bit like citrus fruit combined with the pungent scrub bushes back home that grow where the ocean meets the rocky shore. No doubt some medicine or cleaner, though it did little to instill his faith in this place to heal Violet.

The hospital was made for children; that was evident from the pictures on the wall and the sprightly music playing from some unseen source. The maids, nurses, wore smiles on their pleasant faces and big overshirts decorated with the cartoon characters he had seen on television. They seemed both efficient and positive, and there was little wonder Brianna had brought her sister here for treatments. Sadly, treatments that may or may not be working.

"I'm so glad you came with us, Luke," Violet said.

He tickled Violet beneath her chin and was rewarded with another smile. "I be at your command, sprite."

She narrowed her eyes on him, her mouth quirked. "And Brianna's?"

Luke nearly stumbled. Another glance behind him showed a preoccupied Brianna hadn't heard the little girl's question. Was he at Brianna's command?

He brought his forehead to hers. "Can you keep a secret, sprite?"

Violet looked at him like he was the biggest fool to ask such a question. "Of course."

"If I had my way, I would willingly bend to your sister's will," he said softly. "Forever."

She gave a slow nod, and Luke knew he had this Pixie's trust. If only her sister could be won so easily.

Brianna came up to him then, that false brave smile on her face once more, her eyes shining. "Come, Violet," she said, her tone light.

Luke placed the child on her feet and watched as Brianna took her hand. A flash of blue light, tiny yet unmistakably clear for another Faery to see, connected the two sisters. At Brianna's touch, Violet straightened her tiny shoulders and braced herself. Purposely stepping back, Luke let the two Pixies lead the way toward the place labeled with an odd word he hadn't seen before: outpatient.

Brianna urged her charge along, pushing open a wide wooden door that hid a corridor. Luke saw the place was different here. The long corridor was bracketed by doors on both sides along the way. A few of those cheerful pictures dressed the walls here too, but little noise came from behind each of those tightly closed doors.

A center of activity was straight ahead, manned by another brightly-dressed nurse.

"Hello, Violet!" the round-faced lady beamed.

"Hello," the child answered in a small voice.

"You may take Violet into exam room three, Mrs. Wellbrook." The nurse shot a speculative glance in Luke's direction and faced Brianna again. "Dr. Noble will be with you in a few minutes."

Luke smiled at the nurse when she looked at him again, and her eyes took on that cloudy cast of a woman under his charm. There would be no trouble from this quarter. No questions Brianna wouldn't want to answer nor any impunity to Brianna's virtue.

"I much like your hospital, Violet," Luke said.

The little Pixie merely nodded, all signs of animation dulled now. His hands fisted as it struck him fully: the impotence to affect her condition was so sharp he barely kept himself from doubling over. How the devil did Brianna deal with this over and over again? The woman was stronger than he'd imagined.

***

Brianna steeled herself for another of Violet's examinations as they entered the exam room. The chamber was set up for Violet: stack of oft-read chapter books that wouldn't engage her sister's mind, crisp white sheets that wouldn't give her any comfort, a bag of blessed blood that wouldn't help heal her. So much depended on this visit. She felt it in her soul. The MacDonald following closely behind her did more to ease her mind than she wanted to admit. He had kept Violet engaged during the bus ride despite his own unease and the smiles he coaxed from her with such skill had fairly lit up the world. He didn't know, didn't truly know, all she had endured for Violet's welfare. Oh, he sympathized. For the time being, at least.

Over the past few days, since that first passionate tangle on her little couch, they'd said nothing of the future save for what they would do together the next day. True, Violet's illness had to be her top priority. And while Luke was smitten with the child, his top priority was his family's gold. No smooth words or passionate advances would convince her otherwise.

"I'm scared," Violet whispered.

The tiny voice, smaller even than the little girl, drew Brianna's gaze to Violet. She was pale, her mouth a thin line so different from the curve of a smile she'd worn moments before.

"Don't fret, love." Brianna's own smile felt stiff and false. "Dr. Noble will make it right."

From the doubtful expression on Violet's face, she didn't believe Brianna's promise. She climbed up onto the bed, looking impossibly small as she held her arms at her sides. Luke hung back, but Brianna was grateful for his presence. She sat herself in the hard chair beside the bed.

A nurse soon came into the room, her thin face wearing a polite smile as she efficiently attached the tube to Violet's arm. A glance at Luke showed Brianna his shock, though it was quickly gone. He leaned against the wall and watched in silence while the nurse pricked Violet's finger and drew a droplet of blood into a thin glass tube. Red cell count, Brianna knew. The nurse smiled at Violet, patted her hand and took her leave.

"I couldn't imagine such a thing," Luke said, his eyes large as he watched the blood flowing into Violet. "Does it hurt, sprite?"

That urged a tiny smile from Violet. "Not really."

"The blood should make her stronger, Luke," Brianna said.

From his expression she knew he hadn't missed the doubt in her voice, damn his cunning. The tenderness in his green gaze soothed her pique, however. A shifting around her heart came and her throat tightened. "Luke, I can't tell you how much—"

"Good morning." Dr. Noble came in, fresh and bright in his crisp white coat. He stilled when he saw Luke, and she watched as the two men took each other's measure.

"Will Noble," Dr. Noble said. "And you are?"

"Luke MacDonald."

Suspicion clouded Dr. Noble's eyes, and her glimmer threatened to dissipate. Brianna quickly murmured a few words under her breath and the doctor blinked. He extended his hand to Luke, the friendly smile again on his face. Luke caught Brianna's eye before taking the man's hand in a shake.

"Pleased to meet you, Mr. MacDonald," the doctor said.

Luke nodded. "Noble."

Dr. Noble sat beside Violet on the edge of the bed. He probed her little belly with a thoughtful look on his face. "Hmm."

Brianna watched the doctor's every move, her body stiff. She hadn't realized how much she'd needed Luke until he placed his hand on her shoulder. His strength poured into her like a golden rush and she knew he possessed his own type of magic.

"Doctor?" Brianna asked at last.

Dr. Noble ruffled Violet's pale hair and stood. "I want to wait to see the blood count results, Mrs. Wellbrook. Things are much improved."

A warmth coursed through Brianna, full of hope and cautious relief. She trembled with the strength of it and Luke's hand smoothed over shoulders.

"Isn't my belly smaller, Dr. Noble?" Violet asked. "I

thought so, but I didn't want to get Bri... Mama's hopes up."

Brianna looked at Luke, seeing her emotions reflected in his eyes.

Luke turned to the doctor. "Tell us."

The doctor nodded. "It appears Violet's spleen has at last begun to respond to the medicine. Now she'll need more transfusions, and I don't want you to cease her Prednisone. I'll write out instructions to reduce the dosage over the next few weeks."

"What are you...?" Brianna swallowed and came shakily to her feet. "Are you saying...?"

"The child is better, then?" Luke asked, his voice thick.

The doctor smiled. "It appears so, Mr. MacDonald." He nodded to Violet. "I'll check in on you before you leave today with your Mom's instructions."

Dr. Noble left the room and the door swung shut. In the next instant Brianna was in Luke's arms, laughing and crying against his chest. "She's going to be all right!"

Luke chuckled as he held her tight. "Easy, lass."

She stepped back and wiped the tears from her cheeks. Violet stared up from her position on the bed and Brianna gave her a careful hug, mindful of the tube in her arm.

"Oh, you're getting better, love," Brianna said.

Violet just smiled.

***

The next day was brighter than Brianna had seen since autumn in Cornwall, right before Violet sickened. She longed to tell her grandmother the child would soon be well, but even with her magic she couldn't attempt such contact. And she wouldn't leave Violet just now. She went to the coffee shop to lose her eagerness in the simple, mindless work. Putting some distance between herself and the MacDonald would help her make sense of her feelings, as well.

Last night, after seeing a sparkling Violet to bed, Luke had kissed her good night. Neither he nor she said anything about the gold, but she knew he thought of it. It had wrought a miracle in Violet, aided by the caring staff at the Children's Hospital. Yet Luke's uncle still worsened in Ireland, two hundred years ago. Though the thought made her feel selfish, she longed to keep the gold to see the child's treatments to the last. And to keep Luke by her side. Selfish, selfish, selfish.

"So she's better, then?" Lori asked.

"Yes." Brianna smiled at her friend. "The doctor was pleased. And Luke—"

She stopped, but Lori hadn't missed her slip.

"Luke?" Lori's eyes widened before her lips curved in a smile. "He went to the hospital with you?"

Brianna opened her mouth, finally giving a nod. "He's been wonderful with her. And me."

"I'm glad, Bree." Lori stepped closer and touched Brianna's arm. "You can use someone to lean on."

Brianna didn't want to need anyone, least of all a Braunach from the past who could pop out of her life as quickly as he had popped into it.

"Violet and I are all right on our own, Lori."

Lori clicked her tongue. "Just all right? Don't you want more than that?"

Brianna wouldn't think about it. Sweeping past her friend, she picked up her abandoned coffee pot and stepped in front of a stout man at the counter.

"More coffee?" she asked.

He raised his eyes to her, eyes as black as coal.
Brianna felt her blood chill, and clutched the pot handle
tightly. He said nothing, just stared at her before shaking
his bald head. He hopped off the stool, he was small of
stature, and dropped some coins on the counter. In a flash
he was gone, leaving Brianna to stare after him. She still
shook, so she set the coffee pot down once more.

"Who… who was that guy?" she asked.

"Who, the little guy?" Lori shrugged. "He's been
here a few times in the last couple of weeks. Looks like
Danny Devito, only without the humor. Kinda creepy I
know, but he doesn't say much."

Again, that unease filled Brianna. She thought of the
shifting shadows outside her house the night Luke had
confronted her. Surely Luke had been watching her,
watching Violet. There was nothing furtive about him.
He was as bold as he was confounding, and she admired
that about him as much as his beautiful green eyes or
MacDonald honor.

Luke entered the shop then, wearing the crooked
grin that turned her insides into mush. "Hello, lass." His

175

expression suddenly changed and he took long quick strides to the counter. He took her hands in his. "What's wrong, Brianna?"

She stared down at his hands, so strong and warm, and her worry eased. Lori was right. Having someone to lean on was very tempting.

"Nothing's wrong," she said. "I was woolgathering, that's all."

He didn't believe her; she saw that when his brows drew together. "Is Violet ill?"

"No, Luke." She smiled. "She's quite well."

Luke nodded and sat down at the counter. "Good. I thought we could take her out on the little canal boats in a few days. Maybe one afternoon?"

He offered more of the closeness she was beginning to crave. Why not indulge herself this once?

"It is getting warmer," she allowed. "Yes. She would love that."

That beguiling grin was on his face again. "And you, lass?"

Brianna laughed, at last dispelling the gloom the dark little man had left behind. "And me."

Chapter 14

The afternoon sun glinted off the tiny ripples in the
man-made canal; the breeze was calm and the boat was
sound. Luke watched the two Pixies as they boarded the
little vessel.

An odd boat, it was little more than two bench seats,
the back one separated by a large paddle wheel. As
Brianna snuggled into the seat beside him, brushing her
leg against his, he thought the situation pleasurable.
Violet perched on the bench in front of them and the two
adults began to pedal the boat to less-than-stellar results.

The boat listed to one side. Luke's side, of course.
Their laughter blended in the bright air, and Luke's heart
once more felt that curious pull. Aye, he could lose
himself in these two Pixies; they could become as
important to him as his family back home. Again, duty
gnawed at him. The gold. Always the gold. The
MacDonalds depended on him to satisfy that duty even
as another one drew him.

"This is lovely, Luke," Brianna said.

Her cheeks were pink with exertion and her blue
eyes sparkled. He let the pull take him closer to her,

ignoring the warning bells in his head, the child at his shoulder. They kissed, and she tasted as fresh as the air.

Violet giggled and wrapped her skinny arms around both their necks and planted kisses on their cheeks. The craft rocked and pitched and the three of them laughed again.

Luke knew then. A man could bear the added duty. For this.

He pulled back. "Easy there, sprite."

Violet settled back in the boat, a satisfied glint in her eyes. Brianna blushed deeper, and Luke risked another kiss before bringing his lips to her ear. "You're lovely when you blush, Pixie."

***

Brianna turned and eyed Luke, feeling the draw of those incredible green eyes. He wanted her, as much as she wanted him. As much as he wanted the gold, though? That, she couldn't decide. She thought to simply relish the pleasure his attention gave and swatted his arm.

"Careful with that charm, Braunach," she said.

He grinned and matched his movements to hers, moving the paddleboat slowly up the canal. Brianna leaned back, stretching her legs as she pedaled. This was a day she would remember. The sun and the water. The kisses and the laughter. The ease in passing the time with the man who filled her thoughts nearly every hour.

She glanced over at him and saw that he felt it too, the comfort between them. Amazing, for his closeness usually aroused her senses in a very different fashion since that tangled night on her couch. She pulled her gaze from his and looked at her sister.

Violet had her eyes closed and her arms stretched over her head. Brianna belatedly realized Violet should've worn a hat, but then again the kiss of the sun would do much to enhance her look of growing health. And her sister *was* healthier, Brianna knew that in her heart. Soon the gold would be returned to Luke, what meager amount was left from Violet's final treatments. He would return it to his family in Ireland. Would Luke stay there as well?

"What are you thinking, lass?" he asked.

Brianna faced him, the question in his gaze matching the one in his voice. She couldn't ask him her own questions. Their ease would end in an instant. She lifted

179

her chin and smiled. "I'm simply enjoying the day, Luke."

After a moment he smiled broadly. "Aye, Brianna. 'Tis a lovely day."

The two of them paddled on, reaching the end of the short waterway in companionable silence punctuated only by Violet's exclamations of delight. Brianna inwardly echoed the child's sentiments, taking in the bustle all along the canal steps. People walked along the canal, or stood and drank cups of coffee from umbrella-topped vending carts strategically placed near concrete benches. Brianna sensed the spring fever in the air. And the mortals reveled in the outdoors even if this was a close as they could get to nature in the city.

They managed to turn the boat and returned to where they started almost an hour after they first set out. Luke stepped out of the craft and handed Brianna onto the landing. Her legs trembled from the unaccustomed exertion, but she resisted the temptation to lean on him. He turned back to the little boat and lifted Violet in his arms.

"Thank you, Luke!" Violet said.

He received another hug and smacking kiss from the child, his booming laugh warming Brianna as much as the sun. He drew the notice of two young women walking by the canal and they stopped and whispered to each other before walking closer.

Brianna saw that the weather affected their dress. Their bellies showed and their shorts were so short she wondered how they managed to sit without their bottoms hanging out. She eyed her own clothes, another pair of jeans topped with a T-shirt, and felt decidedly ordinary. Perhaps it was time to use some of her wages to buy a skirt or dress.

The young women stepped closer, their eyes taking in Luke's fine form and handsome face as he twirled Violet in his arms. Brianna saw that Luke paid them no notice, and they soon took themselves further up the walk. She wondered briefly if he'd used his charm here in Indianapolis, to fill his time and his bed. Jealousy struck her hard, and she forced it away. Luke had made her no promises. And she was in no position to ask for any, considering how much she'd asked of him for her sister's sake.

"Are you hungry, sprite?" he asked.

Violet nodded as Luke set her on her feet. He handed her a bit of money, again she was struck by just how clever he was, and the little girl ran ahead toward a cart selling ice cream. He took Brianna's hand without hesitation and she let him. Following behind her sister, she felt a connection lacking since she and Violet had come here. Her heart recognized it. Family.

Luke tapped the tip of her nose and she blinked. "I've kept you too long in the sun, lass."

She shook her head. "I wouldn't have wanted to miss a moment of today, Luke."

He nodded his agreement and twisted her ponytail with one finger. "Perhaps when…"

But he said no more on the matter. And Brianna wouldn't press him to make a promise he couldn't keep.

"There are some lovely gardens near here," she said. "I saw an ad. Would you like to explore them?"

He brightened, no doubt longing for the wilderness he left back in Ireland, back in his time. He lifted her hand to his lips and dropped a kiss there.

"Are you up to visiting the gardens, Violet?" he

called to the child.

Violet smiled through the smear of chocolate on her lips and nodded. Not far from the canals was the White River State Park, the location of gardens unlike any Brianna had seen in what felt like forever. Formal layouts and whimsical collections drew her notice as well as Violet's, and the sense of nature awakening caused Brianna's heart to hope as it hadn't dared before.

Brianna saw to her great delight that the gardens boasted more than just plants and flowers. Butterflies, as beautiful and delicate as any blooms, flew through the conservatory as they carefully strolled about. More than one landed on Luke, a sure sign that his charm extended to animals as well as misplaced Pixies. It was incongruous, a strapping man so gentle with the fragile creatures that he held a pretty yellow one out for her inspection. The rippling fountains situated throughout the conservatory sent up a gurgling sound, the hushed tones of the other patrons added to the sense of sacred nature which spoke to the wild reverence in Brianna's soul. The insect regarded her, its antennae flitting back and forth as she gently stroked its fuzzy body. Large wings brushed up and down in delight and in the next moment it took flight once more.

"You be magic," he said.

***

Luke's gaze held hers and she brought a hand to his cheek, stroking his skin with the same intent softness she had used on the butterfly. Desire filled him, for her body and her soul. The child was off exploring another corner of the place and he took the opportunity to kiss Brianna as he'd wished to on the boat. True, strangers surrounded them in the quiet space. Even so, he could see none save Brianna.

Her body pressed against his and the contact nearly caused him to groan. He stepped back and grinned down into her flushed face. More than the sun had put that bloom in her cheeks. He took her hand and tugged her in the direction of the little sprite, willing his desire to ease as he focused his attention on the lovely hothouse flowers and fluttering insects instead of the temptress at his side.

When they left the gardens, it was still light out though the day was waning. He joined them in their little

184

house for dinner again. Truth be told, he was loath to end their time together. The child held him nearly as much as her sister, though that woman spoke to more than his sense of honor. And after the three of them ate the paper-wrapped sandwiches Luke had bought on their way back, Brianna settled the child down for bed. He sat on the couch and resigned himself to leaving one appetite unappeased.

"Violet's worn out." Brianna quickly shook her head, dispelling his worry before it could fully form. "Oh, the day was wonderful and she's happily tired."

"I'm glad," he said.

The television showed nothing of interest to him, and the Pixie must've shared his opinion for she flicked it off with a wink as she settled beside him.

"I can't thank you enough for today, Luke."

He could think of one way, but he vowed to keep himself from her. Their past entanglements aside, today their closeness was more than he'd imagined. Now his body wanted what his heart craved.

"'Twas my pleasure, Brianna. I enjoyed it as much as the little one."

185

"And the gardens!" Brianna tucked her legs beneath her and leaned against him. "I'd heard of them, but I never imagined such beauty hid in this city."

Luke stroked her hair, willing the other parts of his body to silence as he enjoyed the silken texture beneath his fingers. "You've seen little but the coffee shop and that hospital."

She nodded. They sat in silence, as comfortable as the hours spent before. He began to massage the spot beneath her slender neck and she closed her eyes. Leaning back against his hand, she sighed. Her skin was so soft, her face the picture of pleasure as her full lips curved in an open smile. He kissed her then, deeper than he had dared on the boat or in the greenhouse. And to his delight, she returned it in full measure.

The next instant she was beneath him, her hands stroking his back as she arched toward him. He felt it, passion pounding through him and from her. And he would taste it. He would see her find her pleasure even if it killed him.

Her shirt was scant barrier, as was the silk confection beneath. Her flesh was smoother than the fabric had

186

been, and he gently kneaded her breasts as he kissed her neck, her throat. Her nipples hardened to pebbles beneath his palms.

"Ah, lass…" He took one rosy nipple in his mouth, and the shattered gasp she gave caused him to swell painfully against his jeans. So soft, so responsive. Her hand clutched at his head, stroking his hair as she wriggled against him. He turned his attentions on her other breast, teasing the damp nipple he'd abandoned with his free hand. The other hand eased the fasteners on her jeans loose, and within he found her silken drawers damp with desire. He was nearly unmanned in his own jeans.

"Oh!" she cried.

She arched against his fingers and he slid the thin material aside. She was small, and his finger slowly eased its way inside of her. He stroked her and she fisted her hand in her mouth to silence the cries he knew she longed to make. His own echoed in his mind, and he pressed himself against her thigh as his fingers increased their rhythm.

"Luke, please…"

He found it, the tiny nub of desire swollen and begging for his touch. Covering her mouth with his, he pressed and teased and she shattered beneath him, against him. The lamp nearby flew off its table; the bulb bursting as the room filled with flashes of blue and pink light. He felt her orgasm deep within himself and added his cries to her muffled ones.

Amazingly, he managed to hold on to his control as she softened into the couch. He kissed her again and eased into a sitting position. His head leaned back and he took in gulping breaths as his body hummed with unspent passion. The amber throbbed in tune with his body, with his heart, the leather lace around his neck as tight as his jeans were at the moment. He risked a glance at the nymph at his side, at the perfect body still displayed only for him, and groaned aloud.

She regained herself as she attempted to cover her remarkable breasts with her hands. He suddenly wanted those hands on him, on the flesh that longed to feel all of her.

"Ah, God," he groaned.

Brianna turned and reached for the garment closest

to her, her thin T-shirt. Her breasts were still damp, and the fabric clung to the pink peaks.

"Luke, I never knew such passion," she said.

He took a deep breath and managed a smile. "Nor I, lass."

She fastened her jeans and sat as far from him as the little couch allowed.

"Did I frighten you?" he asked.

She shot him a glance and gave a shake of her head. "No." She looked about the room, at the mess their passion had wrought, and sighed. "I was out of control. That... never happened before."

He bridged the distance between them and pulled her close. "Sometimes you have to let go of your control, Brianna. And I'll take care of you when that happens."

Her lashes momentarily concealed her gaze. "I have your word?"

His throat tightened, words he longed to say lodged securely there. "Aye."

She looked at him again, this time her fair brows drawn together. "But I'm... soiled."

Shame. He heard it clearly and wouldn't stand for it.

189

Grasping her chin, he lifted her face and looked at her evenly.

"Never." He saw it then, the future in her blue eyes. His future. "Brianna, I… What I feel for you, I can't express."

She blinked up at him and finally nodded. "I have your word, Luke. That's enough for now, I wager."

***

"My word, Pixie?" His eyes were dark. "Aye, and more."

He didn't explain. Instead he held her again, peeled her shirt off again and fastened his mouth to hers. She leaned back, relishing his weight against her. He was still hard, and she rubbed against him.

"Ah, Brianna," he rasped.

"Yes, Luke," she sighed. She rubbed her hands over his back, his buttocks. "Yes."

He slid her jeans off her legs and stroked her. Deeper than before, until she longed to have him inside. He shifted and before she could guess what he was going to do his mouth was on her. He murmured to her, his lips humming against her flesh as his tongue flicked over her.

She could only hear her racing pulse as he brought her near to climax again. She knew a moment of fear and he sensed it.

"Easy, lass." He dropped a kiss on her belly. "I'm here with you."

She caught his gaze, green fire scorching her, and licked her lips. He lowered his head again and she leaned her head back as tremors shook her. Then he was kissing her, holding her so close she could hardly tell where she ended and he began. He was still aroused, and she wouldn't let him give without taking anything in return.

She held his face in her hands and smiled up at him. "Let me, Luke."

He let out a soft moan and began to shake his head. She urged him to lean up on his elbows and she reached between their bodies. The angle made it difficult to unfasten his jeans but in an instant he reached down and released himself. He was so big, so hot against her hand. She held him, stroked him as he closed his eyes and rasped her name. His big body shook, his head thrown back as she felt him lose himself against her belly.

He opened his eyes and grinned down at her. "All

right, lass. You may have your way."

She felt her cheeks heat, strange as she was naked beneath him and his seed was slick on her skin. Luke said nothing more of feelings or promises and Brianna was damned if she would ask him for any. His bloody word was all she had at present. That and his passion.

But she couldn't speak of that. Oh, when his lips and hands had worked their own magic, her world had shattered. And when she returned to herself he was there, holding her and whispering words whose intent if not meaning escaped her fevered mind. She suspected she would keep the memory of his earnest gaze forever.

Setting aside thoughts of promises, she needed to see to something else, to make clear one aspect of her and Violet's future.

"What are you going to do about the gold, Luke?" she asked.

He blinked, no doubt surprised by her quick turn of subject. The wonderful day past had allowed the two of them to enjoy themselves for a few hours without the gold dangling in the air between them. And as the air now cooled of their passion, she would have the answers that eluded her these past weeks.

Luke straightened and brushed his auburn locks back from his face before fastening his jeans. She donned her T-shirt again and pulled on her panties. This wasn't the most secure she'd felt in her life, but she had to ask him.

She braced herself for his answer, knowing now that nothing but the truth came from that beautiful mouth.

He faced her. "I must return home."

Her heart stopped at the words and she nodded.

Chapter 15

A time jump. Like before but with a far different purpose. Luke stood in the center of his beige living room, clad once again in the clothes of his time. A white shirt, open at the collar, and tan breeches topping the fine boots wrought to his uncle's standards.

Before he took his leave of Brianna last evening, their passion still humming within him, he'd told her he hoped to see his way clear to keeping the gold for Violet. He hoped that his uncle was on the mend, but he dared not voice his fears on the subject. He would go alone; he wouldn't risk a jump with Violet still so ill and Brianna would never leave the child. Their farewell was sweet. In the throes of his release he might have said something of his growing feelings for her had he not all but bit his tongue.

He grasped the amber pendant in his fist, the disk smooth and cool. A few words, taught to him by Uncle Seamus in a moment of lucidity, and the room appeared to swirl around him. Vertigo caused his stomach to clench and he squeezed his eyes shut to ease the sensation. A loud rushing sound, wind or water or time, roared in his head and he held himself still for the jump. And then… silence.

A few moments later the sound began anew, his skin prickled with hot and cold as the ground rose beneath his feet. It jerked and bucked and he found himself on his backside, his free hand braced in the cool grass beneath him. The world settled and he cautiously opened his eyes. He was home. He had made it and in one piece.

The amber was so hot now it nearly singed his palm. He released it and rubbed his hands on his thighs. He stood and gave a shake of his head. The sound of the birds were the first thing he noticed, then a fading chill in the air signaled spring had come to Meath Province. The smell of earth and growth filled his nostrils. Verdant grass, budding leaves and the musical rushing of a nearby brook combined to bring his senses into focus. Home.

"Luke!"

Luke turned to see Patrick running toward him, a smile on his familiar face. His brother grabbed him by his shoulders and gave a shake. Luke hugged Patrick tightly, engulfed in arms as strong as his own.

"Patrick."

Patrick pulled back, crossing his arms over his chest as he eyed Luke's empty hands. "Do you have the gold?"

Luke bit back a sharp retort. "Do you see it, then?"

Patrick shook his head, his strawberry-blond curls swaying. "Uncle be needin' it, Luke."

That fear of failure bit into him. "Bloody... I know he needs it, Patrick."

Luke strode toward the dell, to the cottage where he and his brothers were raised by their bachelor uncle. Patrick peppered him with questions as he dogged his heels.

"What was it like, Luke?" Patrick asked. "Did you find the Pixie who took the gold? Did she give it up?"

Luke waved his hand in the air, not breaking his stride as he entered the dell. "Not now, pray. I must see Uncle Seamus."

Patrick caught up with him then, and Luke stilled. One look into his brother's face told him all he was afraid to ask. Patrick's blue eyes were clouded, his mouth a thin line. "He be worse, Luke."

Luke spat out a curse. He turned again and walked toward the cottage. It was as he'd left it, odd shaped with additions jutting out on three sides. Three chimneys topped the sloping thatched roof, from the main room and the two bedrooms. Five years earlier Luke had taken himself to his own cottage, built to his uncle's careful specifications. The family remained close, working side by side in the large workshop on the other side of the dell. Patrick and their younger brother, Sean, still live with Seamus, a condition the old man openly bemoaned but nonetheless relished.

Luke entered the cottage, and was struck by the clutter. Their uncle had trained his boys to pick up after themselves, to respect their property as much as each other. By the piles of clothes and books and papers tossed on the dusty wood floor, he guessed Seamus wasn't practicing what he preached.

"What the…?"

"Sean and me, we clean the place every day," Patrick rushed out. "And Mrs. O'Grady does her work. But Uncle… Well, you'll soon see."

Luke nodded and stepped around the mess. "Uncle Seamus?"

A grunt came from the larger of the two bedrooms,

their uncle's chamber. The sound was so unlike the booming voice of the man, Luke's heart sank. He looked at his brother. Patrick's face was ashen, though he'd been living with the man these past weeks while Luke had been tracking Brianna in Indianapolis. Luke walked toward the chamber, bracing himself for the sight of his beloved uncle.

The man seemed smaller, as impossible as that should be. No longer brawny as he'd been, his red hair stood on end. His skin was almost gray, and bits of food clung to his stubble-covered cheeks. His eyes, though... Their vivid green was now as dull as the brackish water in the bogs of Ulster Province.

"Uncle Seamus?" Luke asked.

The man turned his blank gaze on him and Luke's soul nearly froze. No recognition there, none of the affection that normally crackled between the MacDonald men.

"Lucas?" Uncle Seamus asked.

Luke knew he didn't address him, but his father. Dead these past twenty years, Lucas MacDonald and his pretty wife with him. Luke swallowed and stepped into the room. More clothes cluttered the floor here, and the man wore crumpled clothes. They were no longer bright green, and obviously in need of laundering.

"We try to keep him clean, Luke." Patrick's voice was hushed and close to his ear. "But he carries on worse than Sean used to as a babe."

Seamus turned away, dismissing Luke as if he were nothing more than one of the dust motes littering the air in the room.

His heart heavy, Luke turned toward Patrick and urged him from the room before shutting the door. "How long has he been like this?"

Patrick raked his fingers through his hair and sighed. "He's gotten worse over the past week."

Guilt struck Luke. For the time Luke had spent enjoying the company of the two Pixies. And he'd returned home with nothing but hope. There was little good it would do Uncle Seamus.

"Where be the gold, Luke?"

Luke sat at the fine wooden table at the back of the main room, in the dining area. "I don't have it."

Patrick sat down across from him, questions burning

in his gaze. "Did the Pixie use her magic?"

Aye, Luke thought. On his heart, Yes. Not his mind.

"She's strong," Luke said. "And she needed the gold."

Patrick's mouth gaped open. "She…! She needed the gold? What Pixie spell did she cast on you?"

Luke wouldn't speak of it. The time jump had left him tired, and seeing his uncle in such a state did little to revive his spirits. Singing came from his uncle's bedchamber, one of the ditties the man sang to the brothers when they were children. The sound was fey and sweet and nearly broke Luke's heart anew.

"I cannot speak of it now, Patrick."

Patrick just stared at him as he rose from the table. Luke left and made his way to his own cottage. A maid stood outside, one of the lasses he paid to keep his home in his absence.

"You be back, Master Luke?" she asked.

Luke nodded and entered his home. The place smelled fresh and clean and again that stab of guilt struck him. Did his uncle take note of his condition? Did the man realize what he had become? That last possibility caused Luke more pain that any other. For if Seamus knew the level to which he had fallen it would surely break his proud MacDonald heart.

The maid, a plump girl nearly more than marriageable age, hurried into the cottage. She bobbed a curtsey—red-faced because she'd neglected to do so earlier, he assumed—and fluttered about the kitchen.

"You've food in the larder, Master Luke," she rushed out. "And me mum be wantin' me back to see about the family chores."

"Go, then." He didn't remember her name. "And I thank you. The place looks well."

She curtseyed again and picked up her rough-hewn bag. "I'll be 'round in the mornin'."

Luke didn't argue, suspecting that his spirits would be little improved when the sun rose and he wouldn't trouble himself with housekeeping. She left, closing the door behind her.

He let the silence engulf him, tears burning his eyes. How ill his uncle looked; how desperate his brother was. He rubbed at his eyes and let out a breath. He had family who needed him here and now. And family back in the future as well.

"Ah, Brianna."

He closed his eyes, picturing her fair features and sparkling eyes. Last evening he had nearly taken her, there in her snug borrowed little house. Passion so hot, sweet in her release, innocent and seductive as she brought him to release. And she had asked nothing of him but the passion. That and the bloody gold. He could only leave her with hope he'd keep his word. Bloody hope. He wasn't any closer to a resolution as he had been in that haze of waning passion there in her arms.

Luke rose from the table and opened the larder. Plenty of foodstuffs, and fresh bread set on a shelf. He took the loaf and a hunk of good cheese back to the table and began to eat. It was simple fare, lending itself well to contemplation. The ice box held some fresh milk; no doubt the girl kept the place stocked as he'd indicated he didn't know when he would return. He would have to reward her. All he had was the money from the future, and that was back in his flat in Indianapolis. No gold here to pay; he hadn't considered that. Little surprise there. Fine ale also stood at the ready, and he took the jug to the table.

A sharp rap came on the door and Luke groaned softly. He could well guess the identity of this visitor.

He rose and opened the door, finding Sean as he'd expected. The baby of the MacDonalds at twenty-one, he nonetheless resembled both Patrick and Luke. Darker than either Luke or Patrick, he possessed the same green eyes as Luke. Those eyes flashed with anger and hurt. The boy still held no rein on his emotions then. Luke had thought that a failing. Before Brianna had taught him to let go.

"Where be the gold, Luke?" Sean asked.

Luke leaned against the doorjamb. "And how are you this fine afternoon, Sean?"

Sean waved a hand through the air and stepped around Luke into the cottage. "Patrick fed me some bit about a Pixie charming you out of the gold. 'Tis our gold, Luke!"

"I bloody well know it is, Sean!"

Sean recoiled at Luke's outburst. He recovered quickly, however.

"And yet you come back with nothing?" Sean asked.

"Surely she wasn't as good as all that."

Luke felt his blood boil at the insinuation. He stepped closer to Sean, his height giving him the advantage he needed. "What are you sayin', brother?"

Sean shrugged. "Cornish Pixies be right bonny, Luke. Takin' her favors while—"

Luke's fist smashed into his brother's face. He pulled his punch just in time, but still managed to knock his little brother to the floor. "You'll not speak of her that way!"

Sean propped himself up on one hand and rubbed his jaw with the other. "You are bewitched."

Luke laughed without humor. "Not as you might expect, Sean."

He held out his hand and helped his brother to his feet. Confusion eclipsed the anger on the boy's face.

"But… you saw Uncle Seamus?" Sean asked.

"Aye," Luke said. "And it pained me greatly."

Sean blinked. "Then you know you must bring back the gold."

The temptation was there again, to flatten his baby brother.

"I know my duties well, Sean. As I told Patrick earlier."

Sean pouted. "He didn't say anything about you hittin' him."

Luke smiled. "You pushed me harder than he did, brother."

Luke waved his brother to the other chair at the table as he sat once more. Sean joined him in an ale, his dark brows drawn together.

"You found the gold," Sean said.

Luke waited a beat.

"Aye," he said.

Sean drank deeply of his ale. "And the Pixie had it."

Luke took another bite of bread and chewed.

"Aye," he said.

Sean clasped both hands around his mug and stared into its depths. "I don't understand."

Luke raised his mug in mock-salute and drank. "Neither do I, brother. Neither do I."

Sean left soon after, puzzlement still clear on his face. Voices reached Luke at his self-imposed solitude, the sounds of families gathering at their homes, returning from work to comfort. An ache began in the center of Luke's chest, and he suspected more than one cause for it. Ah, Uncle Seamus had made a wonderful home for him and his brothers, but it now seemed like the family was slipping away. And Brianna was leagues and years away, and the comfort found in her embrace was gone from him as well. Would his brothers understand about the gold? Would they care about the tiny Pixie so ill and in need? And what of Brianna? Both his brothers thought she'd charmed him, Patrick with her magic and Sean with her passion. He pictured her eyes, her smile. Her body, her touch. Damn them to hell, they were both right!

The sun was down for hours when Luke at last succumbed to the lure of the bed set in the room behind the kitchen. He removed his boots—he missed his sneakers, he thought fleetingly—and stripped. The downy counterpane, wrought by the ladies of the dell who took it upon themselves to see that the boys had some mothering along with Seamus's guidance, brought physical comfort at least. Luke would have to wait for the solution to his dilemma for any true comfort. Perhaps on the morrow…

Chapter 16

Luke rose with the sun. He stretched and when his hand brushed the rough wall he gave a start. What the…? Opening his eyes, he saw he slept in his own home. Gone were the colorless bed linens and nondescript artwork that filled his bedroom in Indianapolis. So he was here, then. In Meath and facing a duty he'd rather avoid. His family wouldn't allow that, though. Neither would his conscience.

He swung his legs over the side of the bed, and his muscles groaned in protest. The bed wasn't to blame. Nay. His sleep couldn't have been poorer if he had slept on the wide plank floor. And the day was only just beginning.

He washed and dressed, thinking to go to his workshop before visiting his uncle again. He frowned into the mirror above the washstand. Coward.

Sean and Patrick were able cobblers. And surely business hadn't suffered with his absence. True, all in the dell—and to some distance out of it—relied on MacDonald shoes and boots. Seamus had made a good name for the family as well as a good home.

Luke ate some more bread, a bit hard but passable. He grabbed the milk from the iced box and choked some down. He missed his daily coffee, not to mention the Pixie who served him so prettily in Indianapolis. Not much coffee to be found here in Meath, and he wouldn't travel to Dublin for the brew. He took two apples to appease his hunger. He missed the food of the future, the crunchy sweet cereal. As he munched an apple, he left the cottage and made his way to the workshop.

"'Mornin', Master Luke!"

Luke nodded to the round baker who waved from the door of his shop. More Meath inhabitants waved or called their greetings, but Luke didn't pause in his stride. They would ask about his uncle. And about the gold. Few secrets were kept in the dell.

When he reached the workshop his brothers were already within.

"About time you showed up, brother," Patrick shouted from his workbench.

"Takin' to livin' the easy life in the future, eh?" Sean chimed in.

Luke rolled his eyes and chose to ignore the barbs.

209

He looked about the shop, seeing that some work had piled up while he was away. His brothers appeared to have the business in hand, for the most part.

The smell of fine leather and saddle soap filled the air, along with the gentle and steady tapping of careful hammer on tiny nail. The MacDonalds were known for their quality of workmanship, and with good cause. Even after weeks of sitting in the back of his closet in Indianapolis, his own boots still fit him like a second skin.

"Place looks good," Luke said.

Patrick and Sean grunted their thanks, barely looking up from their tasks. Patrick polished a pair of fine boots, and Luke noted the bright green color. His stomach dipped. Patrick crafted the fine footwear for their uncle.

"They're very fine," Luke said.

Patrick nodded and took a step back, wiping his hands on a cloth. "Thought Uncle Seamus would see them and… remember."

So much in that statement, spoken in a husky tone. Luke clapped Patrick on the shoulder. "Is he alone?"

"Nay. Mrs. O'Grady minds him while we work."

Luke watched his brother's hands skillfully work the hammer. "It's been hard while I've been gone."

Patrick shrugged. "Aye."

"Work's been a help," Sean said from his bench.

Luke gave a nod. "Good." He gave a cursory glance about the rest of shop, finding little to delay his progress. "I'm off to see Seamus."

Sean met his gaze, his eyes damp. Luke left the workshop, bound for his uncle's cottage.

Luke rapped on the door of the cottage, gaining an answer he hadn't been expecting.

"Come in, come in!" his uncle boomed.

Luke opened the door and found the man seated on his velvet chair, a wing chair built to his specifications and covered in velvet of his favorite green. Though his clothes were rumpled, they appeared clean as did his face and hands. His red hair curled wildly about his head, but that wasn't so far from its normal condition. Luke dismissed all those details when he looked into Seamus's eyes. They were as clear a green as a prized emerald.

"Luke, my boy."

Luke grinned and shook his uncle's offered hand.

The grip was weak, but he wouldn't think about that. "How are you, Uncle?"

"Fine." The older man appeared puzzled, his head cocked to one side. "Why do you ask?"

Luke wished for his brothers' company at the moment, to question them about this perplexing recovery. From the sounds coming from the kitchen, he knew Mrs. O'Grady worked in there. Everything seemed fine, as it had before.

Luke sat down on the settee across from his uncle, resting his elbows on his knees as he leaned forward. "You feel well, then?"

Seamus laughed, a hearty sound. "Fit as a fiddle and twice as noisy!"

Luke smiled at that. "But I thought without the gold you would—"

"You found our gold?"

Luke gave a slow nod. "Aye. It's where O'Shey said it was."

His uncle's mouth turned down. "O'Shey, the vile Leprechaun. Don't trust him, Luke. He'll be wantin' something for helping us."

Any day now, Luke suspected. Leprechauns were not known for their patience.

"Aye," he said.

"So you brought back the gold, then?" his uncle asked. "Your brothers will be happy."

"But what of you?" Luke asked. "I thought you needed it."

Seamus laughed again, that wonderful sound of mirth so long missing, and Luke's heart jumped in response. His eyes glinted with an understanding that escaped Luke. "Not only gold be a treasure, my boy."

"Uncle, what…?"

But the man was gone, in mind and spirit. The change was so abrupt, it left Luke breathless.

"Lucas, you marry the girl," Uncle Seamus said. "She loves you."

Luke grasped his uncle's hand, desperate to bring him back. Not the man he was when Luke's father courted his mother. Nay, the gentle man who had sat before him a moment before. Lucid and clear and sharp.

"Uncle Seamus!" Luke said.

"Love be the most important thing, brother," Uncle

Seamus said to Luke's long-dead father. He withdrew his hand from Luke's after giving him a reassuring pat. "Thirty years I've wasted, but don't you do it. Love will keep you when all else is gone."

Before Luke could question him further the singing began again, that high-pitched childlike song that deeply chilled him. Seamus rocked back and forth in his favorite chair, his arms wrapped around his drawn-up knees. The sparkle in his eyes, the direct manner of speaking, was gone. *He* was gone.

Luke swallowed around the lump in his throat and struggled to his feet. "I'll... I..."

His uncle didn't seem to notice either Luke's words or actions. He was gone to that place again, his self and dignity lost because of the gold.

"Mrs. O'Grady," he called.

The lady stepped out of the kitchen, wiping her hands on the apron across her wide middle. "Aye, Master Luke?"

Luke flicked his head in Uncle Seamus's direction, not that subtlety was needed in this case. "Pray, look after him?"

The woman nodded. "Aye. 'Tis my duty since you be gone."

Innocent words, spoken in earnest. They struck him in the heart. Since he'd been gone. Gone. He'd left his family to reclaim the gold, to heal his uncle's mind. And he'd returned with nothing.

"Aye," he said and headed for the door.

He had to bring the treasure back somehow. Had to satisfy Violet's treatments as well. No answer seemed clear but he wouldn't find it here, watching his uncle deteriorate. And he couldn't face his brothers' disapproval. They were right, damn it.

Uncle Seamus had spoken of love, when he thought Luke was his father. Surely that explained what he meant by thirty years. Luke didn't dare hope his feelings for Brianna would prove the answer. He would go back to the future, though. To Brianna.

***

Brianna wiped down the counter, another dull day at the coffee shop behind her. Lori asked after Luke yesterday but, after Brianna's evasive answers, she didn't pester her about him. Brianna shook her head. If only

Violet were as accommodating. The child was so
determined, but she had only asked what Brianna herself
wondered.

"Hey, Lori!" a masculine voice called.

Brianna looked up to find Luke's friend Jim had
arrived. Lori leaned over the counter and the two shared a
kiss. Brianna blinked. How long had the two of them
been seeing each other? The past weeks, first spent in
hiding and then in company with her tracker, had
obviously clouded her mind to anything else.

As Lori went in the back to get her purse, Jim waved
in Brianna's direction.

"Hey, Bree," Jim said. "Have you seen Luke?"

She shook her head in honesty. "He's... visiting his
family."

Jim nodded, accepting her answer. He smiled and
gave her a wink. "Not that I've seen much of him lately."

Brianna flushed hotly. As oblivious to her friends'
business as she had been, she hadn't realized they would
know of hers. Not that she and Luke could hide the
attraction that flowed between them. A pang of
loneliness struck her, deep in her core.

"Y-yes," she said.

Lori returned and the two of them bade her good night. Brianna retrieved her sweater. She called good night to the boy cleaning in the kitchen and stepped out into the evening.

It was still light out, not that she ever felt in peril on her walk home. The protection spell still served her well. The hairs on her nape shivered just as she had that thought, quickly dispelling her sense of safety. She whirled, seeing nothing behind her nor to the left or right. Her key was still, though it only seemed attune to Luke's presence. And he was far away in more ways than one.

She hurried home, unable to shake the feeling that someone was watching her. And if her senses were to be believed, danger was closer. When at last she closed the front door behind her, she breathed easier. "I'm home, Mrs. Henning."

"Hello, dear."

"Hello, Brianna!" Violet called.

Violet sat on the couch, piles of books surrounding her. One of the house's previous tenants must have much enjoyed reading. And that was fortunate because now that she spent far less time sleeping, Violet was quickly making her way through the volumes.

"How was your day, love?"

Violet shrugged. "Nothing much to do, except read and watch the telly." She gave a start and looked intently at Brianna. "You're sad."

Brianna attempted a smile, but her sharp little sister saw through the weak expression.

"I'm fine, Violet." Brianna stood and straightened the blanket thrown over the back of the couch, work meant to keep her hands busy and herself away from Violet's too-knowing gaze. "So you feel better, then?"

Violet snorted. "You can't hide it from me, Brianna."

Brianna finally looked at her sister. She gave up the fight and sat beside her on the couch.

"I miss Luke," she said.

Violet wrapped her arms around Brianna's neck and gave a squeeze. Brianna took the comfort, her eyes tearing.

"He'll come back." Violet stroked Brianna's hair, the same gesture Brianna used to soothe her during her treatments. "He'll come back for you."

Brianna closed her eyes and prayed her sister was right.

Chapter 17

The carpet was scratchy beneath Luke's palms as the room stopped spinning. The amber around his neck cooled and he opened his eyes. He was back in Indianapolis and, though he was closer to Brianna, he was no closer to solving his dilemma. And he would have to tell her all of it. She'd accept nothing less.

Luke changed out of his old clothes and donned jeans topped with a soft collared shirt. A quick glance in the mirror showed he was in need of a shave, so he saw to that and stepped into his favorite pair of sneakers. He would grab something to eat at the coffee shop; he couldn't delay the inevitable.

Uncle Seamus was worse than when Luke left him weeks ago. His brothers couldn't reach him most of the time, and surely the man would soon become a danger to himself. Despite Brianna's compelling reason for it, this was all because she took the gold. What the devil was he to do now?

He opened the door to leave, startled to find someone standing there.

"Hello, MacDonald."

Luke blinked as he looked down at the familiar, ugly face. Daniel O'Shey of Ulster Province. Had the imp follow him from Meath?

"O'Shey." Luke let him in and shut the door. "Why are you here?"

"To get me share!"

Daniel sat on the couch, his legs folded beneath him. He gave less thought to his attire than Luke apparently; he wore tattered jeans and a faded T-shirt, both items no doubt cast-offs from some unknown mortal here. The modern shower apparently held no interest for the Leprechaun. He stunk like a bog in August.

Daniel regarded Luke closely, his black eyes sharp.

Luke had nothing to give the Leprechaun, but he wouldn't let him know that. Not yet. "It'll be a while, O'Shey. I don't have my hands on the treasure yet."

Daniel chortled. "Oh, ya' have yer hands on the Pixie though!"

Luke fisted his hands at his sides. "What do you know of it? You just—" At Daniel's grin, Luke knew. "You've been following me."

Daniel waved a pudgy hand in the air and hopped off

the couch. "Aye, though ya' were sure slow about it. She be pretty, the Pixie. I can see why ya' took her to yer bed."

Luke's hands fisted. "I never took her to my bed! And you'll not be speakin' so of her, O'Shey."

Daniel shrugged. "I care not who ya' bed, MacDonald. I told ya' she had yer gold and she does. I want me share and then we'll return to Ireland."

Luke raked his fingers through his hair. How the devil was he to get himself rid of Daniel?

"How did you follow me before?" Luke asked.

Daniel rolled his eyes. "'Twas easy. Just as ya' fell to the ground I touched yer boots."

"But you weren't here when I arrived."

"Ya' landed near the busy streets, MacDonald. I hid in an alleyway till ya' left."

The alleyway? Something tickled at the back of Luke's mind. A few times he was certain he sensed something. Had Daniel been following him all along? My God, had he followed him to Brianna's?

"I won't have the gold for a few days," Luke began, his mind working. Daniel was cunning. Not as sharp as a

Braunach from Meath, though. "You'll have to give me a chance to take it from the Pixie."

That slick grin came again. "Seems ya' took plenty from her."

Luke didn't rise to the bait. He crossed to the door and held it open. "Where are you staying?"

"Got me a room." He looked around the flat. "Ain't as nice as this place, though. Ya' must have some of yer uncle's money, then."

"Aye." Luke took a breath. "Do you need any?"

Again, those dark eyes sparkled. "I be hungry, and the food here be pricey. Except for that little shop where the Pixie works."

Luke withdrew some paper money from the pocket of his jeans and thrust it at Daniel. "Here. And stay away from the Pixie else you won't get a another farthing from me."

Daniel's round face turned red. "Ya' owe me, MacDonald! Don't be makin' me wait!"

"You'll have your share, O'Shey. A Braunach keeps his word."

Apparently, Daniel missed the slight toward the

Ulster Leprechauns.

He nodded with satisfaction and clutched Luke's money in his chubby fist. "Yer time be runnin' out, MacDonald. Pray, have an answer fer me. And soon."

With that, the imp left. Luke slammed the door and spat out a curse. Daniel O'Shey followed him from home weeks ago! And he no doubt watched Brianna once Luke was foolish enough to lead him to her. What else did the little man know? Did he know of Violet's illness? Surely he'd seen their house. He'd know the gold was hidden there as well as Luke did.

No reasonable argument would work with a Leprechaun of Daniel's clan. And Luke wouldn't risk exposing Brianna and Violet to the bastard by divulging the truth of the little girl's plight. If his opponent would only fight fairly, Luke wouldn't hesitate to send him back to Ireland. Daniel wasn't to be trusted, and his clan's legendary lust for gold surpassed any rational thought. So reasoning with the imp wouldn't work, either.

Luke left the flat, bound for the coffee shop. He needed to see Brianna, to make certain Daniel hadn't touched her in his absence. If Daniel knew of the passion they'd shared, surely he'd watched the house more intently than he divulged. Damn him to Hell!

Brianna was soon before him, bustling behind the counter as she served the patrons seated there. Again he was struck by her honor, and the knowledge that she hadn't used a bit of the stolen gold for her own luxury or comfort. And now he had to take what little was left of the treasure in hopes of appeasing Daniel O'Shey? What would happen to Violet? To Uncle Seamus?

"Brianna," he said.

She looked up, and as he saw the love shining in her gaze he once more heard Uncle Seamus's declaration of that emotion's value. *Love will keep you when all else is gone.* If only he could believe that.

***

Brianna stilled as she drank in Luke's appearance. Had he only been gone for two days? Her body reacted sharply to his presence; her heart pounded and her face flushed. He smiled at her, but it was a faint expression compared to his usual grin. She knew in her heart something terrible had happened back home. And it would soon befall Violet as well.

225

"Luke," she said.

He stepped closer and sat down across from her. She reached for him and he grasped her hand in his. His eyes spoke to her heart, and she sucked in a breath.

"I have to speak with you, Brianna," Luke said.

She swallowed and pulled her hand away from him. "I can't." She looked at the customers waiting her service and chose to see them for the escape they represented. "I'm very busy."

Lori called to her, flicking her head in the direction of the door. "I'll see to your customers, Bree."

Brianna didn't know whether she should thank Lori for the consideration or dig in her heels and refuse to leave the coffee shop. She reluctantly untied her apron and handed it to Lori as she passed her.

Luke waited for her at the door and waved her ahead of him. No words were spoken until they gained the little alleyway behind the shop.

"Brianna, I…" His eyes glistened with tears.

She brought her hand to his cheek. "Tell me, Luke."

He clutched her to him, his body shaking with silent sobs as he buried his face in her neck. "He didn't know me, Brianna. My uncle is gone."

Brianna soothed him, stroking his head as he steadied himself. He released her and took a step back, swiping at his eyes. "Forgive me."

She waved that comment away. "What are you going to do?"

He shook his head. "I don't know. Perhaps he… My uncle spoke to me, Brianna. For a moment he seemed himself. Then he… he didn't make much sense."

"He's ill, Luke." Her stomach dipped. "And it's all my fault."

His brows drew together as he gave a violent shake of his head. "You had no choice, lass."

She turned from him, wrapping her arms around her waist. "And now what?" she whispered.

She heard him, his feet shuffling on the walk as he stepped closer. He didn't touch her. And that told her much.

"I'll find a way, Brianna," he said. "Perhaps what he said… Ah, I don't know."

She faced him again, this man who had come to mean so much to her in such a short time. So noble, so devoted to both his family and hers.

"Maybe Violet is strong enough now," she said.

Luke's eyes widened. "She must stay here, lass. Your Dr. Noble said as much."

Brianna brushed her hair out of her face. "I know, I know. If your uncle needs what gold is left—"

"Nay!" he shouted.

He grabbed her arms and his intensity coursed through her.

"You did this for her," he said. "She's nearly better and she must remain."

She kissed him with all she had in her. He pulled her against him and she was nearly lost. Something niggled at the back of her mind, the notion that soon he would leave her and never return. Despite his words, his family needed him; his uncle no longer led the family and that duty would fall on Luke.

Brianna wrenched out of his arms, trembling as she sought to find the strength that had served her well since coming to this place. Little of it remained as she stood there, sensing all at war within him. The crystal key vibrated, low and deep. She turned and took a few steps away from him.

"I must get back to work," she said.

"Brianna, wait."

"Luke, leave me be."

A muttered curse came from behind her as she continued on her way.

"Brianna!" he called.

She didn't turn. She couldn't face him any longer. There in his eyes she'd seen the certainty that he would take the gold and leave her and Violet. Despite his honor and his bloody word!

***

Luke watched her go. The Pixie was smart, and attuned to him. His senses still tingled from her reaction to his feeble arguments. She knew he needed the gold, though he'd promised her he wouldn't bring a halt to Violet's recovery. And now there was Daniel O'Shey, the dark devil. Daniel wanted his share, a portion of the gold not already gone to the doctors for Violet's care. Would Luke be able to help his uncle with so scant a treasure that would be left?

He couldn't speak to Brianna. Not now. His heart

aching, he made his way back to his flat to find a way to best Daniel. He suspected a solution to his problem with Brianna wouldn't be so simple.

***

The pub was noisy, the hour growing late even for a Friday evening's amusement. Luke sat at the long crowded bar, nursing his tankard of thick ale. Daniel perched beside him, drinking deeply of his brew.

"I ain't been here before," Daniel said. "Seen ya' come in here with that mortal, though."

Jim. Thankfully that man hadn't pressed Luke this afternoon. He'd asked Luke to join him and Lori, and to bring Bree along to make it a foursome. Luke had declined the invitation, but his good-natured friend had suspected nothing. Luke didn't want to expose anyone to Daniel, so he brought the imp to a different bar than the one Jim and Lori planned to visit tonight.

"Aye," Luke said. "Tasty brew, isn't it?"

"Aye." Daniel slurped and wiped his mouth on the back of his hand. "Brings home to me mind, it does."

Luke waved to the skinny waiter flitting about the pub. The pretty young man stopped at their table and gave Luke a look he was used to getting from the females of Indianapolis.

"What can I get you, Brawny?" the young man asked.

Luke blinked at the carnal invitation in the boy's eyes. His cursed charm worked on mortal males now?

"I…" Luke swallowed. "Another ale for me and my friend, pray."

The waiter pursed his lips. "Ooh, love that accent!" He placed his hand on one slim hip and sighed. "All right, handsome. Be right back!"

The boy danced off and Luke dismissed him from his mind. Daniel eyed the waiter with confusion on his face, finally giving his head a shake.

"Fey, that one," Daniel said. "He be a fairy, ya' think?"

A mortal on Daniel's other side laughed out loud and slapped him on the back. "Good one!"

Luke waited for him to say more, but the man paid his bill and made his way toward the tables. The waiter returned with the ales and, after another flirting glance at Luke, left them alone.

"Ya' got me gold yet, MacDonald?" Daniel asked.

Luke reined in the urge to grab Daniel's fat neck and pound his face into the bar. He clenched his hands around the tankard instead and shook his head.

"I told you I need time, O'Shey." Luke turned to face him. "And here I thought you'd want to share a nice evenin'."

The dose of charm worked and Daniel nodded. "Aye, been lonely. Ain't had the pretties all over me like you and that mortal."

He glanced around the bar and Luke followed his line of vision. More than one woman eyed Luke, but that wasn't out of the ordinary. When he looked back at Daniel, he saw the envy there.

"This place isn't like home," Luke said. "The lasses here be different."

An ugly smirk curved Daniel's lips. "I be wantin' to find that out."

Luke waved to the skinny waiter again as Daniel drained his ale. He gestured for only one refill, at which the boy gave an exaggerated wink and did his bidding. 'Twas going to be a long night.

Chapter 18

Brianna tucked the comforter around Violet's slight body, taking care not to wake her. It was after midnight, and yet she couldn't find her own sleep. The encounter in the alleyway preyed on her mind. Luke needed the gold, and so did she. He hadn't asked for it back, but she was no fool. It was a mess, and she couldn't see how even Luke's cunning could find a way out of this. Not for all of them.

She brushed an errant lock from her sister's forehead and rose from the bed. The bloody key in her pocket gave a flutter, but she chose to ignore its meaning. She was bone-tired, and a faint headache thrummed behind her eyes.

Lori had questioned her after she'd spoken to Luke, but thankfully the woman hadn't pressed her for any answers. And when Jim arrived as they prepared to close the place, he too asked after Luke. Luke and she were joined in the eyes of these mortals, then. Why not? They were joined in Brianna's heart.

She readied for bed at last. A cold splash of water on her face eased her head a bit, and she donned her nightgown and reached for her key. As she touched it, it began to tremble. She heard it then, a soft scratching at her front door. She slipped the key's ribbon around her wrist and left the bedroom.

Taking cautious steps, she approached the door. She braced herself to use all the magic at her disposal to keep the danger at bay.

"Brianna?"

Soft as a whisper, Luke's voice reached through the door and wound itself around her heart. She opened the door and he rushed in.

"I had to see you, Brianna," he said. "To make you understand."

She closed the door and crossed her arms over her chest. Anger filled her. "You want the gold."

"If only you would let me explain," he said.

Brianna paced the length of the living room, back and forth and back again. Her hair floated about her and the lights flickered.

"You want the gold, Luke. Don't deny it!"

He reached for her but she eluded him. As difficult as this exchange would be, she had to keep her distance.

If he touched her…

He smiled his crooked grin and a warmth coursed through her. "I need only a portion of it, lass."

"Luke, I…."

"Come, Brianna," he said. "I just need enough to—"

"Oh!" Brianna gave a shake. "Don't try to charm me, MacDonald. You want me to free the treasure from my spell and then you'll take it all!"

She fought to ignore the wounded look in his eyes.

He splayed one hand on his chest. "I would never do that to Violet. I thought you trusted my word."

Brianna laughed without humor. "Your word. Yes, your bloody word! Yet here you stand, attempting to charm me out of my sister's only means of getting well?"

He growled as he raked his fingers through his hair. "I need the gold, Brianna. Just a portion, pray. If he doesn't get it—"

"However would your uncle mend with just a portion, Luke?" she asked. "I don't believe you for a moment."

He grabbed her then and her body felt on fire. Anger and passion and indecision made her dizzy.

235

"Not my uncle, damn it," he said. "Listen to me!"

She couldn't. She wouldn't. "No. You come here, so bloody arrogant and pressing me to release the gold to you. You charm me, I daresay. You'll not have me again."

He dropped her as if he felt her fire. "You don't understand. Ah God, you won't understand!"

He stormed from the house, and after a moment Brianna ran to the open door.

"Luke, wait!" she called.

But he stalked away from her. And out of her life. She closed the door and fell back against it, tears choking her throat.

Brianna came awake with a start some time later. Something moved in the center of the house, something stealthy and shuffling. She glanced at her key, but the crystal was dim and quiet. Not Luke then, though he had entered her house without invitation that one night. That night of passion and of truths. She shook her head. Or so she had believed.

She eased out of her bed, donned her terry robe and tiptoed down the hall. The room was dark except for a shaft of light peeping through the curtains from the streetlamp in front of the house. She felt a chill and turned toward the bookcases. A figure stood there. Crouched, really. Small and round, dark and quiet. Recognition slammed into her in the next moment. It was the little man from the coffee shop!

"You there!" she cried.

He whirled on her, his black eyes catching the meager light from the window. Those eyes chilled her, void of warmth and compassion. She now knew him for what he was: a Leprechaun.

"Hello, Pixie!"

He laughed. The sound made the hair on the back of her neck stand on end.

"Get out of my house," she said.

He shook his head. "Nay! I want me share of the MacDonald gold!"

Then she knew. Luke needed the gold to appease this imp. He had kept his word. Her own hurtful words came back to her. How she wished she hadn't sent him away. No matter. She would face this threat alone if she had to. For Violet's sake.

"It's not here," she said.

He laughed again and stepped closer. "Lyin' Pixie, are ya'? Nay! MacDonald told me ya' have it."

She crossed her arms, seeking to show as strong a presence as she could muster. "You can't have it."

He shook with anger, vile curses spilling from his mouth. "Give me the gold!"

He lunged for her and she raised one arm, sending him flying into the bookshelves. Shaking his head, he stood once more.

"Yer magic be strong, Pixie," he grumbled. "But I'll get me share."

He made for her again. Flashes of light filled the living room as she threw all of her power into ridding her house of the devil. He dodged her attacks, moving with a speed that belied his portly appearance.

"You won't win, imp!" Brianna cried.

Tiny fires smoldered on the carpet. Windows shattered but still he evaded her.

He laughed and came closer still. "Now I be havin' a taste of what the MacDonald sees in ya'."

She knew he tried to use his cunning, but his

intelligence was far beneath Luke's. Why wouldn't he fall?

Brianna murmured the words for the strongest lightning spell she knew, raising her hands over her head to deliver the blow she prayed would stop him at last.

"Brianna?" Violet whispered.

Brianna turned her head as Violet entered the room. "Violet, don't—!"

A flash of pain at the back of her head caused the room to spin. She tried to keep her balance, and as she fell the sound of Violet's scream was the last thing she heard.

***

Luke walked toward Brianna's little house, the sky still dark. It was too early for such a call, but he needed to see her. After leaving her last night, he'd gone to his apartment. When he'd left Daniel at the pub, deep in his cups, he'd hoped to gain Brianna's cooperation. Now, after a fitful night's sleep, he knew that would be impossible. She thought him so mercenary as to take Violet's chance at recovery? He set aside his anger at her rash judgment. Well, he'd make her listen to him now.

239

As he got closer to the house, something struck him as odd. Several windows were broken, and the acrid smell of smoke filled his nostrils. His heart pounding, he ran up the steps and rushed through the open front door.

The light from the streetlamp was enough to see the damage. The living room was in shambles, the carpet singed in spots. Most of the furniture was broken and there were books all over the floor.

"Brianna?" he called.

No answer. He made his way through the wreckage toward the hallway. "Violet?"

Still no answer. What the devil happened here? Perhaps Daniel hadn't been as drunk at Luke presumed. And if he came here…

Something caught his gaze before his mind fully formed the horrible possibilities: a stocking foot peeping from behind the couch.

"Brianna!" He found her unconscious, her face pale. She sprawled on the singed carpet, limp and boneless. No! He took her in his arms and gently stroked her cheek. "Wake, lass," he said. "Please wake."

He felt her arms and legs and found no injuries. One

touch to the back of her head showed him the reason for her condition: a large lump raised on her scalp.

He held her close, willing her to wake. At last his amber began to warm against the base of his throat and she stirred.

"Violet?" she whispered.

That one word told him more than he wished to know. God, don't let it be so.

"Brianna, lass." He kissed her cheek. "It's me. Luke."

She opened her eyes, clouded but beautiful. "L-luke?" She struggled to sit up. "Where's Violet?"

He shifted to give her some room. "I don't know, lass." He grasped her chin and made her face him. "Brianna, tell me what happened."

Tears filled her eyes, but he knew the pain in her head wasn't the cause.

"He came here, Luke," she said. "A Leprechaun. He must have… Oh God, he must have taken her!"

"We'll find her, Brianna."

She sniffled, gazing up at him.

"Do you give me your word?" she asked.

He smiled gently. "You trust my word, lass?"

She gave a nod. "I should never have lost faith in you, Luke."

***

Brianna felt the effect of her words in her heart. Luke's eyes shone with love, though she'd refused to see it for anything more than passion until now. He kissed her gently and eased her to her feet. Something struck her then.

"The gold!" she cried. "Oh, please don't tell me he took the gold!"

She ran to her bedroom, Luke's heavier tread close behind her as she pulled open the closet door. Kneeling before the closet, she closed her eyes spoke the spell that revealed the gold. The wall shimmered and her face warmed. When Luke took in a sharp breath, she knew her words had their effect.

"The MacDonald gold," he murmured.

She faced him and saw the awe in his eyes. "I used a lot of it for Violet, Luke," she said. "I'm sorry."

He took her hand in his and dropped a kiss on it. "A noble cause, lass. Thank you for keeping it safe from

O'Shey."

She nodded.

He turned her hand in his, looking closely at her wrist. "Did the bastard tie you? I didn't see any ropes when I found you."

On her wrist was a faint red mark, most likely caused when the devil tore her key from her. Oh, no.

"He took the key, Luke."

"Your key?"

"My grandmother's crystal key!"

"Your grandmother's…? What are its powers?"

She couldn't tell him it vibrated whenever his fine self came close to her. Surely he would find that strange and believe her daft.

"I used it to come here from Cornwall," she said. "She said it also… She said it had hidden powers as well."

"O'Shey won't know how to use it, I wager," Luke said. "But he'll crawl back to whatever comes closest to his home."

Brianna nodded and settled on the couch. "His home? Oh, Ulster?"

Luke nodded gravely. "Aye, Ulster. Damp and cold on the warmest summer day."

"But where in Indianapolis could he find such a place?"

"I don't know," he said. "I'm a good tracker but we'll need your magic, lass."

"This is all my fault." Brianna buried her face in her hands. "If I hadn't sent you away tonight—"

"Nay, Brianna! I thought the devil deep in his cups. Bloody bastard's built like a bull." He sat beside her and took her into his arms. "Pray, don't cry. We'll find her."

Chapter 19

Brianna concealed the gold with a wink and they returned to the living room. She faced Luke as they stood among the debris. The anger on his face echoed her own. And he wanted to find Violet as much as she did. That touched her heart more than the love she thought she saw in his eyes.

He pulled the collar of his shirt aside to show her the amber pendant and Brianna stepped closer. The pendant was beautiful up close, and as she gazed at the stone it began to glow. Luke's eyes flickered with the same warmth.

"Touch it, lass," he said.

Brianna reached out and fingered the amber. It pulsed in response to her touch and Luke blinked.

She stilled. "Does it hurt?"

Luke gave a quick shake of his head and smiled crookedly. "Nay."

She closed her hand around the pendant and it seared her palm. It didn't hurt, just a tingle that coursed up her arm. Luke closed his eyes and gave a start, obviously feeling the electricity that flowed between her and the stone. They were connected, she, Luke and the stone, and it felt so right.

She focused her mind and murmured the spell that would help her find Violet. The amber grew hotter. Suddenly she saw the place, dark and dirty and cold. Big looming shapes, low buildings or trucks, she couldn't tell. Long metal tracks, stretching and twisting over the ground. She could smell the acrid scent of fuel, hear a faint whistle through the mist or fog. She'd seen Violet though, huddled against a filthy wall in one of the structures. Her sister was frightened and cold, and her soft cries echoed in Brianna's brain. Fog clouded Brianna's "vision," though she suspected it was the place that was blurred and not her mind. She felt her sister's fear, her worry, to her core.

Brianna's heart clenched and the amber grew so hot she had to release it. "Violet!"

Strong hands grasped her arms and she jerked back to herself.

"Brianna," Luke said.

She opened her eyes and she was in her home once again. In Luke's arms once again.

"I saw the place, Luke," she whispered. "I saw Violet."

He uttered a blessing and gazed heavenward. "Thank God, lass. Where is she?"

She shook her head. "I'm not sure. There were lots of buildings, low and close together. That can't be right, though. The place was dirty and cold and… foggy, I think."

Luke looked thoughtful, finally shaking his head. "'Tis nothing to me. There be few buildings in Ulster. Aye, but it *is* cold and dirty."

Brianna sat on the couch and Luke joined her, holding her hand tight in his.

"The feeling was… close, like there were lots of them," she said. "Wait! There were lines of metal tracks. Train tracks." She faced Luke. "There were train cars all around her, Luke. I think she was inside one of them."

"Poor sprite." Luke shook his head. "These… trains pass through the city all the time, don't they?"

She nodded again. "Yes. I think he took her to where there are lots of trains, though."

"You'll have to be tellin' me where," he said. "I've

no notion of trains."

She knew he was right. Now was her time, but she didn't know the area around Indianapolis any more than she had when she first arrived months ago. She was as lost as Luke in this. Her heart sank.

"Oh, I don't know what to do," she murmured. "How will we find her?"

"Jim."

"Jim?"

"Aye, lass." Luke wore a smile on his face. "Jim will know where these trains are."

"Brilliant!" She hurried to her room, stepping over the debris her battle with Daniel had left behind. The fight had done no good and now Violet was trapped, held by that devil. Her hands began to shake. "Just…" She swallowed. "Just let me get dressed."

"Brianna," he said.

She stopped in the hallway and turned to him.

"Dress warmly," he said.

His touch of concern was the last she could take. She sank to the floor in the hall, her arms wrapped around her knees. In an instant Luke was beside her, holding her and stroking her as she had done to Violet so many times during her illness.

"Shh," he soothed, kissing her hair, her cheek.

Brianna cried now, fat tears that soaked Luke's shirt. She could feel his heartbeat against her cheek and she let herself sink into his strength. "God, please let us find her well."

"We shall, lass." He held her chin in his hand as he had before and gently wiped her cheek. "We shall."

He helped her up and she dressed, a smile twitching at the corner of her mouth as she donned a sweater. There was so much to him she hadn't realized. Charm and cunning, yes. Strength and heart, too. She shook her head. She didn't have time to entertain thoughts of love at the moment. Violet was her concern and would remain so. Just please God, let her still be alive.

They stepped onto the porch and Brianna turned to lock the door.

"The windows are open, Brianna," Luke said.

She let out a breath. "I know. But your gold, Luke."

"'Tis under the spell."

She latched the door and pocketed the key. Again

she thought of the crystal Daniel had stolen. Would he be able to use its magic?

"The gold is concealed now," she said. "But if anything were to happen to me—"

"Nay!" Luke held her arms. "Don't say it."

"If the spell was broken, Luke, anyone could steal it."

Luke released her and ran his fingers through his hair. "Aye."

"Your gold is too important to lose."

He suddenly smiled and her heart jumped at the sight. "You called it 'my gold,' Brianna."

She smiled. "It is, isn't it?"

Luke took her to his apartment building, close to the canals where they'd ridden in the paddleboat. He negotiated the glass elevator with practiced ease. He impressed her yet again; he was smart enough to get along in a time and place so different from his home. Well, they needed his strength and cunning tonight. With his charm and her magic, they had to find a way to best the vile Leprechaun who took her sister.

***

Luke glanced at Brianna as they rode up in the glass box to his apartment. He had closed his eyes when she placed her hand on his amber, his senses tingling. He'd watched her as she went to Violet in her mind. Such anguish had twisted her features it had nearly broken his heart. And the worry was still visible, though he'd coaxed a smile out of her on the porch.

"'Twill be all right, lass," he said.

She leaned against him and he held her close. Like before in the hallway, as her tears had soaked his shirt, this felt right. *They* were right and they would get Violet back.

"I pray it will," she said.

He kissed her, a gentle kiss to wipe away her frown. The metal wall slid open and they stepped out into the hallway. He passed his own door to go further down the hall. A glance at his watch told him it was nearly four o'clock in the morning. No matter. He'd forget the manners Seamus had taught him just this one time and call without prior announcement.

"Here's Jim's door." He rapped on the door.

He took Brianna's trembling hand in his as he waited

for his mortal friend to answer, stroking her palm with his thumb. No answer came from the other side so he knocked again.

"All right!" he finally heard from inside the apartment. Shuffling footsteps toward the door. "Who the hell is it?"

Luke glanced at Brianna. "It's Luke."

The door opened and they found a rumpled Jim standing there, his fair hair mussed and his lids heavy.

"What's up, Luke?" He noticed Brianna and his brows raised. "Bree?"

Luke ushered Brianna into the apartment, an exact replica of his own temporary dwelling, and closed the door. "We need your help, Jim."

"My help?" Jim rubbed his face and nodded. "Right. My help. What do you need?"

Luke reined in his impatience. "We need to know where the closest train yard is, Jim. Do you know?"

"The train yard?" Jim asked. "Here in Indy?"

Luke glanced at Brianna again. She was wringing her hands.

"We need to get to the train yard right away, Jim,"

Luke said.

"Well, I don't know much about anything but downtown." Jim glanced at the closed bedroom door, close to the living room. "Hey, Lori?"

Luke and Brianna exchanged a puzzled glance. Brianna's mortal friend opened the bedroom door. She was also tousled from sleep but appeared quite comfortable in one of Jim's large shirts.

"Jim, what are you—?" Lori blinked at them. "Bree?"

Brianna went to her friend. "We need your help, Lori. You've lived in Indianapolis a long time, right?"

Lori nodded and yawned behind her hand. "About five years. Why?"

"They need to know where the train yard is, honey," Jim said.

Lori spared a smile in Jim's direction before facing Brianna again.

"What happened, Bree?" she asked. "Oh! It's not your little sister, is it?"

"It is," Brianna said.

"Oh God, she isn't worse, is she?"

Brianna shook her head. "No." Her voice cracked but she held her shoulders straight. Pride filled Luke at that moment. Aye, she was a worthy lass.

"Do you remember that dark little man, Lori?" Brianna asked.

"From the coffee shop? Yeah." She gave a shudder. "Always creeped me out a little, with his black eyes. What does he have to do with your sister?"

"He took her," Luke stated.

"What?" She looked from Brianna to Luke. "Why?"

They couldn't tell these mortals the truth, not now. Jim and Lori wouldn't believe them, anyway. They didn't have time for a lengthy discussion of Leprechauns and time jumps.

"I… We can't say," Luke said. "But we believe he took her to the train yard."

"Did you call the police?" Lori asked. She pointed toward the phone on the desk. "Jim, call 9-1-1."

"Nay," Luke said quickly. "They can't help."

"Why not?" Jim asked. "This makes no sense."

"Pray, don't press me, Jim," Luke said. "There is no time to get them involved. Brianna can find her."

"All right." Jim turned to Lori. "Do you know where the train yard is, honey?"

Lori sat at the table and rubbed the sleep from her face. After a few moments she lifted her head. "That would have to be west of the city."

"Would it be foggy there?" Brianna asked.

Lori shrugged. "Sure it gets foggy. The land kind of dips down in spots and it's been cold at night."

"No wonder the imp took her there," Luke said.

The mortals both looked at Luke in question, but he shook his head. "Where is it?"

Lori told them which road to take out of the city and to go west. "Just stay on thirty-six and you'll run right into it. It's just south of the thirty-six."

"I'll drive you," Jim offered, grabbing his keys from a bowl on the counter.

"No," Luke said. "We'll not involve you in this."

Lori looked at Brianna. "She's in danger, Bree. Why won't you let us help you?"

"Thank you, Lori," Brianna said. "But no. Luke's right. The danger would be greater for you both. I promise we'll explain later." She looked at Jim. "May we borrow your car?"

"Yeah." Jim gave Brianna the keys. "The car is on the second level, near the back. A silver Nissan."

Before they left, Lori gave Brianna a hug. "You'll find her, Bree," she said. "Luke will see to that."

Brianna nodded and looked at Luke. "I know."

The faith in her eyes nearly knocked him to his knees. Luke prayed he could live up to it.

Chapter 20

Brianna drove Jim's car, a luxury edition probably furnished by his employer. It took her some minutes to adjust to driving on the right side of the road. Luckily traffic was light at four o'clock in the morning.

Luke sat transfixed beside her, his eyes on the lights and gauges on the dash. She smiled a bit at his awe.

"A little different from the carriages back home, I take it?" she asked.

He met her gaze and smiled. She felt that now-familiar jump in her heart.

"Aye," he said. "'Tis true I'm glad you're driving."

So was she. She gripped the steering wheel tightly, the lacing around the leather-wrapped wheel biting into her palm. "It helps to keep me focused, I admit."

He gently touched her hand and she felt his strength. She relaxed her grip.

"We'll find her, lass," he said.

She looked at him again, at his green eyes bright with MacDonald honor. "I pray we will."

"O'Shey is no match for the two of us."

"You know him, Luke." Brianna swallowed hard

257

and gave voice to the fear that had been in her mind since finding Violet gone. "Would he… Would he hurt Violet?"

Luke gave a shake of his head, his face fierce. "Nay. He's a greedy bastard but a coward, too. I don't think he'd try to hurt a Pixie of Violet's power."

Brianna raised her eyes heavenward. "Thank God she's recovering." She forced her focus on the road. "I don't know what she can do to him, but hopefully she's strong enough to make a protection spell."

"She's your sister, Brianna." He winked at her. "Nothing would surprise me."

She nodded and drove up to a traffic light that had just turned red. Tapping her fingers on the wheel, she gathered her strength. This was a long time coming, but she owed him this much.

Finally, she looked at him. "I'm so sorry about the gold, Luke."

"Never mind that now, lass." He placed his hand at the back of her neck. His capable fingers worked her tense muscles, stroked her shoulders. "We'll sort it out later."

It was there again in his eyes, his love, his nobility.
She wished she could surrender all her worry, all her
responsibility. The beep of a car horn behind her brought
her out of her reverie and she moved forward beneath the
green light. "Yes."

She wouldn't give voice to the fear that when all was
done he'd have little to save his uncle and she'd have
little of him.

The city was soon left behind. Strip malls and
grocery stores took the place of tall buildings. Brianna
could *feel* Violet, could feel herself drawing closer to her
sister. They reached the city called Avon, which made
her think briefly of her beloved England. This place,
more stores and gas stations interspersed with dark,
empty corn fields, bore no resemblance to home. She
soon spotted it, the sign directing them to the train yard.

"Turn there," Luke said.

Brianna jerked the wheel and turned left, going south
of the highway. The sound of clattering wheels and
whistles broke the silence.

"She's here, Luke." Once more Brianna had to force
herself to loosen her grip on the steering wheel. "I can

feel her."

The train yard was a vast place full of engines and freight cars. Fog blanketed the yard, thick and yellow in the light from the street lamps. Brianna swallowed her fear and glanced over at Luke.

Where would O'Shey hide Violet? Luke was silently observing the place, his eyes narrowed. She could almost feel his cunning. She prayed he would find her.

She pulled off of the main road onto a gravel one. The tires crunched over the rutted road, the car rocking back and forth as she pulled to a stop. She killed the engine and turned to face Luke.

***

Luke caught Brianna and pulled her to him. She trembled for a moment and he stroked her back. "It's time, lass."

She nodded and closed her eyes. As he watched closely, she sensed the place with her powers. Her eyes drifted closed and she stiffened. He could do nothing but continue to watch, tamping down his own worry.

This place of trains was strange and quiet. Metal tracks wound over the scrub covered dirt, some holding train cars, some glinting in the half light. The yard felt close and tight, as close as the bogs of Ulster. It was dark and cold and dismal. A fitting place for the bastard O'Shey. But what of sweet Violet?

"She's so scared," Brianna said.

Her voice chilled him, soft and low. Again she trembled. Suddenly her eyes snapped open and she clutched his arm.

"She's here, Luke." Her gaze darted out the front window and she glanced quickly around the place. "But I don't know… Where is she? My magic is as clouded as this bloody fog!"

"Easy, lass." Luke took her shaking hands in his and rubbed them. "We'll find her." Perhaps if he kept saying it, it would be so.

He helped her from the car and they stood on the gravel, each of them searching for some sign of O'Shey or Violet. The ground shook beneath his feet and he braced his legs apart. Trains moved along the tracks just west of where they stood, and the grind of metal on metal echoed eerily in the thick night air. He forced himself to hold on, to let Brianna focus on her sister and not his unease.

He took Brianna's hand in his again and dropped a kiss on her knuckles. "Search for the key, lass." He wrapped her fingers around his amber. "I pray this will find it."

She gazed up at him, her blue eyes glistening from the moonlight and her tears. Her fingers stroked the stone and for the second time that night he felt the jolt once more. She closed her eyes again and he studied her beautiful face. He saw her brow furrow, saw her mouth purse. Then she brightened, releasing the amber.

"You saw her, lass?" he asked.

"She's over there," she whispered. She pointed toward overgrown tracks and boxy shapes. "Where those abandoned cars sit, Luke. I saw her!"

She ran but he caught her and held her hand. "You can't be chargin' in there, Brianna. And if your magic is affected by this fog…"

She muttered an English curse and he almost smiled.

"I'll need you, Luke," she said. "Your cunning."

He felt the faith she had in him and was humbled. "Not my charm?" he teased.

She let out a breath and gave him a grateful smile. "Let's go."

They crept toward the train car Brianna had indicated, their hands still clasped tight. He wasn't going to let her go. Not now. As they drew closer, he could hear someone pacing back and forth on the rotting boards, creaking and knocking. He could hear someone muttering and cursing, and Luke knew it could only be Daniel O'Shey.

Violet's voice, soft yet strong, reached him and his heart leapt. Brianna jumped beside him and he was glad to be her anchor in this.

"Quit yer muttering, ya' damn Pixie!" Daniel shouted.

Ah. Violet wove a protection spell. His Brianna had taught her sister well. Once again pride filled him. He shot a look at Brianna and she spared him a nod of understanding.

"Violet is safe for now, lass," Luke whispered. "We can attack the bastard without worrying over her."

She nodded again. They went around to the back of the train car, keeping their footfalls as quiet as possible on the gravel. He said a silent prayer of thanks for his sneakers as they made their way.

They came up to a gap in the boards forming one wall and pressed their faces against it. Luke smelled the dankness, the scent of smoke. He peered inside.

Violet sat in one darkened corner, her eyes closed as she continued to chant her spell. She rocked back and forth and Luke could see a shimmer of a bubble around her. *That's it, sprite.* Beside him, Brianna shook as she gathered her strength. Luke released her hand and stepped back. She aimed her power at Daniel and let loose with a shot to shatter the boards in front of them.

"Ow!" Daniel jerked, his hair standing on end. "Son of a whore! Who—?"

Luke tore through what was left of the rotting board and charged at him. Daniel was quick, damn his hide, and dodged his attack. Brianna struck again, and the floorboard beneath Daniel shattered in a flash of light. Again, the imp escaped. His laughter filled the train car, low and sly like Daniel himself. He grabbed Violet, yelping as her touched shocked him, and held her like a shield.

"Ya' found me, ya' bloody Braunach." He narrowed dark eyes on Brianna. "The bitch hid yer gold."

"Let the child go!" Luke shouted.

"Nay!" He cowered against the wall, still holding tight to the child. He flicked his head in Brianna's direction. "She be me protection against that one!"

Brianna shook, her hair a halo about her as crackling sparks lit the space. She raised her hand toward Daniel and Violet but Luke stopped her.

"Nay, lass." Her eyes, huge and bright, settled on his face. "Your magic… Here…"

Brianna nodded, fisting her hands at her sides. She faced her sister and silently mouthed her name. Violet's eyes locked on Brianna's and Luke stepped back. A blue light flashed between them and their powers united. Like at the hospital, Luke saw the link between the two as a living thing. Pixie to Pixie, sister to sister. Daniel didn't stand a chance against the two of them.

Violet shook free of Daniel, moving so fast Luke barely registered her escape. In the next moment he took the opportunity it afforded and dove toward Daniel.

Stronger and larger than the Ulster Leprechaun,

Luke still had difficulty subduing him. Daniel fought like the devil, vile curses spilling from his mouth as he writhed and kicked at Luke's legs and stomach. At last Luke grabbed Daniel's thick neck in his hands and throttled him until he went slack. Luke dropped him and straightened.

He took in deep breaths as his pulse slowed at last, resting his hands on his knees. He wrenched the crystal key from one of Daniel's slack and grubby hands. The thing was tiny in his palm, with a fragment of blue ribbon still clinging to it. It pulsed a blue light and Luke blinked. He rolled it around in his palm. Something about the key reminded him of something, the cuts in it looking as if it might fit—

"The key, Luke?" Brianna asked. "Is it all right?"

"Aye." He turned to find Brianna and Violet in a tight embrace. Again that shimmer filled the car, this one light and sharp and wrapping around the two of them. He crossed to them and waited, hesitant to break them apart.

"Brianna," he said.

She looked at him, her eyes shining. He knew they were tears then, tears of relief and gratitude. He knew it because he felt them on his own cheeks.

He glanced down at the carved crystal key in his palm, at the soft blue and pink glow pulsing within. He held it out to her. "Your key, lass."

Brianna took the key he offered, closing her hand over the trembling crystal. She relaxed her shoulders. "Thank you."

Violet touched Brianna's closed fist and turned toward Luke. "Thank you, Luke."

Luke swallowed hard. He crouched down and she wrapped her arms around his neck. He hugged her back, as tightly as he dared.

"'Twas your sister's work, sprite," he said. "She found you."

Violet leaned back from him and pulled down the collar of his shirt. "Of course she did." She pointed at the amber and it pulsed a beat. "She had this."

Luke looked at Brianna in confusion, but she just blinked in confusion.

She tucked the key into her pocket and took Violet's hands in hers. "We have to get you home, love."

Violet yawned and nodded. Her eyes rounded. "Isn't

Luke coming?"

He stared at her for a long moment before answering.

***

Brianna's eyes stung with tears as the answer struck her. He wasn't coming.

"Nay, sprite." He pointed a thumb in the Ulster Leprechaun's direction. "I have to be gettin' this vile creature back home."

Violet, bless her, only believed part of his story. Brianna wouldn't ask him what else drew him away. She couldn't bear it.

"What of your gold?" Brianna asked.

Luke smiled that crooked grin that always made her heart race. She fisted her hands and kept her expression impassive.

"You need it for the sprite, lass," he said. "You keep it here. For Violet."

Brianna longed to hold on to Luke, to pressure him to stay here and now. Her heart knew. She loved him. She hadn't told him, but she loved him! She knew he had to return to his home, damn his bloody word. To his family.

"Brianna, I…" he began.

She shook her head. The key seemed to voice its disagreement as he stepped closer, humming and jittering in her pocket. She wouldn't give in to the temptation to throw her arms around his neck as Violet had done. To bury her face in his neck and smell that scent that was uniquely Luke. It's better this way, she told herself. Pity she couldn't believe it.

"Thank you, Luke," she said.

He hugged her, wrapped her in his arms and she let a tear slip from beneath one lid. So strong. So pure. Her heart knew it.

"We'll meet again, lass," he said.

He rubbed his chin on the top of her head and she resisted the desire to snuggle closer.

"You have my word," he rasped.

He gave her a gentle kiss and released her. His word. Brianna watched as he gathered the fat little Leprechaun in his arms. He straightened and stood in the middle of the wrecked train car and clutched his amber. He swayed as the amber glowed bright and then, with a whoosh, he was gone.

Brianna's breath caught. "Good bye, Luke." Brianna glanced at Violet. The little girl had tears on her smooth cheeks.

"He had to go, Violet," Brianna said. "We… We'll be fine."

"It's not fair," Violet murmured.

Ha, fair! Brianna said nothing to that. She helped her sister down from the train and led her back to Jim's car. She sat behind the wheel and closed her eyes. After silently wishing Luke a safe return home, she started the car.

Her urgency gone now, and with her sister dozing safely beside her on the leather seats, the ride back downtown seemed to take forever. She knew the real reason she wasn't in a hurry to get back to the city. It had nothing to do with the mess in her pretty little house or the work awaiting her in the coffee shop. No, her heart knew the real reason. Luke was no longer there.

Chapter 21

"This be the bastard who took the gold?" Patrick asked.

Luke shook his head to clear it, his ears still echoing with the sound of wind and time. He eased up from where he'd landed after his time jump and brushed his hands on his thighs.

He glanced up at Patrick. What was his brother was doing in the clearing at this ungodly hour? That was beyond him at the moment, so he dismissed Patrick's rumpled appearance and faced him.

"Nay, Patrick," he said. "This be the vile Leprechaun who told me the Pixies took the gold."

Patrick's lip curled. "Ulster, I wager?"

"Aye."

Patrick ran his eyes over Luke. "What you be wearin'?"

Luke looked down and saw he still wore the clothes of Brianna's time. In his haste to get Daniel O'Shey as far from Brianna and Violet as possible, he hadn't even given a thought to leaving his clothes and boots in Indianapolis.

O'Shey groaned as he came awake, sending those inconsequential thoughts from Luke's mind. The fat Leprechaun opened his eyes. He cringed as he saw Luke standing above him.

"Nay, MacDonald!" Daniel cried. "I gave up the little lass!"

"What's he talkin' about, Luke?" Patrick asked.

Anger filled Luke as he hadn't allowed back at the train yard. The bastard had touched Brianna, had taken Violet! He grabbed Daniel and hauled him to his feet.

"Shut up, O'Shey!" Luke growled. "Or I'll do what I should have done back in the train yard."

Daniel's lips closed tight and his eyes went round.

Luke gave a snort and turned to his brother. "This piece of filth kidnapped the Pixie's little sister, Patrick. And sick she was, too."

Patrick blinked in surprise before glaring at Daniel. "Bastard."

"I couldn't be gettin' yer gold," Daniel whined. "The bitch hid it from me."

Luke saw red. "Watch that vile mouth of yours, O'Shey!" He gave Daniel a violent shake. "And no more excuses, you worthless sot." He faced Patrick again. "I will take him back to Ulster, Patrick. He'll dare not trouble the MacDonalds again." He gave Daniel another shake. "Will you, O'Shey?"

"Nay, nay!" Daniel's nose ran as he began to shake. "The Pixie be havin' yer gold now."

"The Pixie?" Patrick asked. "Still, Luke?"

Luke didn't have time to explain, not now. "Later, Patrick," Luke said. "I've a disagreeable task ahead of me and 'tis almost morning."

Patrick scowled but asked nothing more as he followed behind Luke. Luke dragged Daniel to the stables and bound his hands with a rope, leaving him crouched in the straw.

"Pray, watch him while I change," Luke said.

"The Leprechaun wouldn't dare make a move while a MacDonald watches him, Luke." Patrick crossed his arms, mirroring his brother's stance as Daniel cowered. "Will you, O'Shey?"

"N-nay," Daniel whispered.

Luke gave a nod. He strode quickly to the tack room and withdrew a spare set of clothes he kept there. He

273

stashed the clothes from the future away, carefully folding the comfortable clothes before setting them atop the fine leather sneakers. He wished he could set aside his memories as easily. That he could tuck them neatly away to look at another day.

He had to focus on the task ahead. To give thought to his wishes now... Nay. He didn't have that luxury.

Returning to the stables, he nodded to Patrick. "Thank you, brother."

He dragged out the cart and he and Patrick harnessed their sturdy gray horse. Luke settled his captive on the boards, and not too gently. Daniel moaned and groaned over his position but the brothers ignored him.

Luke climbed up on the seat, clenched his teeth and gave the reins a tug. "I'm off."

"'Twill be a long ride, Luke," Patrick said.

Luke simply nodded.

As Luke finally reached Ulster, the sun was coming up behind him. He rolled his shoulders, rocking a bit to ease his sore backside. Thankfully for the past hour or so Daniel had dozed, snoring loud enough to wake the birds in the trees overhead. Luke preferred the snoring, however. Daniel's incessant wheedling and cajoling and whining and begging had done little to improve Luke's mood. Foul imp.

Much weighed on Luke, more than the task immediately before him. Soon Daniel wouldn't be his concern any longer. There was still the matter of the gold, though.

He knew it was safe in Brianna's care. What of his uncle? Patrick didn't have to tell Luke; he knew in his heart Seamus was still sick in his mind. Luke's heart ached. It wasn't the loss of the gold or even the prospect of losing his uncle that caused him so much pain. Aye, he knew the reason. He loved Brianna and now he'd lost her forever.

Luke slowed the cart as they came into the square. "Get up, O'Shey."

The little village was waking. Smoke curled from chimneys and he could see farmers out in their fields to the south. Luke trusted the Ulster clan to see to Daniel's justice. A greedy lot, nevertheless they were rumored to possess a kernel of honor Daniel never showed. Luke set his shoulders. 'Twould be to the MacDonalds they would answer if they dared not see Daniel punished.

One round man, his head barely covered with white hair, exited the nearest building.

"Ho, there!" Luke called.

The Leprechaun bustled over to the cart. He blinked small eyes up at Luke. Recognition crossed his face. "MacDonald?"

"Aye. Luke MacDonald."

The little man glanced at the petulant Daniel curled up on the floor of the cart. "Daniel O'Shey? Ye be a miserable excuse for a Leprechaun."

"Aye," Luke said again. "And you can have him."

The old Leprechaun clicked his tongue. "What mischief he be gettin' into, MacDonald?"

"He kidnapped a child."

Luke knew the simplest statement of Daniel's crimes would be the most effective. All Faery folk valued children, be they fey or mortal. He need not mention she was a Pixie.

The man gave a grave nod. "He'll not be troublin' anyone for a long time, Luke MacDonald." he said. "Ye have me word."

Luke took the man's offered hand and stilled. He fixed a glare on the Leprechaun, who trembled under his gaze. When he nodded again Luke gave one strong shake and released him.

"Aye," he said.

He dumped his cargo on the muddy road and didn't spare Daniel another glance.

"Daniel O'Shey, you piece of offal," he heard the old Leprechaun begin. "Ye be payin' for yer crimes, ya miserable…"

Letting out a breath, Luke turned the cart around and headed for home.

Home. How odd he had come to think of Indianapolis as home over the past weeks. Nay, he corrected himself. He had come to think of Brianna as home. She was where he belonged. And now she was gone from him. Centuries away. And he was here.

"'Tis foolish to think on it," he muttered.

He drove the horse on toward Meath and the troubles ahead of him. The luxury of thinking of other matters— Brianna, Violet, love—was far from him now.

***

"Luke will come back, Brianna."

Brianna fingered the woven blanket covering the back of the couch. The worn fringe flowed through her fingers. She couldn't give voice to the hope Violet's words put in her heart. She released the threads.

She shook her head at her little sister. "No, Violet. He has responsibilities back home in his own time."

Violet crossed her arms, her lips pursed. "But Grandmother said—" She snapped her mouth closed. "Never mind." She peered down at the open book in her lap. "You'll see."

Brianna studied Violet's bowed head. The little girl couldn't fool her for a moment. The edges of several pages fluttered as if of their own accord but the child wasn't reading.

"What did Grandmother say, Violet?"

"What? Oh, nothing I can recall." Violet looked up with a pretty little pout on her lips. "I was quite sick when we left, Brianna."

Brianna clicked her tongue. "Never mind. Why don't you read that book you've been studying so hard, love."

Violet blushed as she laughed, the pages of the book

278

fluttering as she lost herself in the pages. It was funny that the child took such delight in a book about a boy wizard.

Brianna sat beside Violet, close for her own comfort. She was uncomfortable to be away from her sister even for a little while. The ordeal of the last night still weighed on her, the drain on her power, the heart-stopping fear when she'd awoken to find Violet gone. Perhaps if she'd been stronger, the imp wouldn't have been able to take her sister away with him. Never had she felt such terror. If not for Luke…

When she'd awoken in his arms, before the blinding panic had struck, she'd been filled with a sense of rightness. She wouldn't think about him. Not now. He was home, and no wishing or casting of spells would bring him back by her side.

Violet had another treatment on Monday, and Brianna had another payment to make. Guilt gnawed at her. She still had Luke's stolen gold, and he still needed it back. She prayed, evoking a power stronger than Pixie magic, to ease Luke's way and heal his uncle. She doubted her powers could stretch two hundred years in the past.

She closed her eyes and let her head fall back against the couch. Lord, she missed him. His laughing eyes and charming looks; the strength of his honor and the depth of his passion. The way he held his own passion in check until she'd found heaven in his arms. She loved him. And there was nothing to bridge the distance between them now that the gold would soon be gone. How could he ever forgive her for taking his uncle's chance while giving Violet hers?

It took plenty of her power to right the house once they'd come back from the train yard. Books were on shelves, lamps righted, windows fixed. The place was neat and clean but it felt so empty. Even with her sister snuggled so close beside her, Brianna still felt so very lonely.

Violet had slept through much of the car ride to Jim's apartment, a relief to Brianna as the child couldn't see how much her hands shook on the steering wheel. He had driven them back to the little house, all the while peppering her with questions about Luke. The brief answers she'd given him had done little to ease his curiosity. No doubt Lori would pester her for answers when she saw her at the coffee shop on Monday morning. At least she had time to concoct some story to appease her friend. She wouldn't use a glimmer, not on someone who'd proven loyal and trusting with little information except for what Luke and Brianna had given them.

Brianna brushed back a silken lock of Violet's hair, tucking it behind her ear. After sleeping the clock around, the little girl appeared none the worse for wear. Amazing. Violet's magic must be nearly back to full strength if she'd been able to keep the Ulster Leprechaun at bay for the hours it took Luke and Brianna to find her. Perhaps they wouldn't have to use all of Luke's gold to see her to full health. Perhaps she could reserve some of it for Luke. Then he could return to her and— No.

"If only that could be," she sighed.

"Hmm?" Violet asked.

Brianna shook her head, never opening her eyes. "Nothing, love. Go back to your story."

Violet said nothing more. Tears stung Brianna's eyes but she fought them. She wouldn't cry in front of Violet.

The last thing she needed was for the child to take it upon herself to see matters set to rights. And the Lord only knew what the little Pixie might do. That caused a corner of Brianna's mouth to lift.

She opened her eyes and withdrew the crystal key from her front pocket. It was silent, the stone facets dull and colorless. Funny, but when her grandmother had given it to her back in Cornwall, its color had been like this. Since the first moment she'd seen Luke, though… She shook her head and pocketed the stone.

"What do you want for dinner, love?" Brianna opened her eyes. "Some pizza?"

"Oh, pizza would be lovely."

Brianna stood, unable to resist dropping a kiss on her sister's brow before heading into the kitchen to call for pizza delivery.

***

"It's me, Uncle Seamus." Luke took in a breath, tamping down his frustration as he heard himself say the same sentence yet again. "It's Luke."

As before, the man said nothing intelligible. Seamus chanted in that eerie sing-song voice and stared off in the distance. Whether he looked at the past or the future, Luke couldn't guess.

Uncle Seamus had been like this since Luke came back from Ulster, a shell of himself. Sunday at Mass in the chapel on the square, Seamus had sat like a stone. No lilting voice added to the hymns, no strong rumble speaking the prayers they all knew by heart. Luke had been able to escape Patrick and Sean's interrogations following the service, but he knew that particular luck wouldn't last for long. And his brothers had every right to learn what had happened in Indianapolis. He was a coward to hope to delay their questions any longer. Thankfully the two younger MacDonalds weren't here with Luke and Seamus. Patrick and Sean had gone into the kitchen and were no doubt driving Mrs. O'Grady daft as they tried to sample whatever tasty dish she made for Sunday dinner. Nay, Luke had to face his uncle alone.

They sat in Seamus' parlor, neatened by Mrs. O'Grady while they were away at Mass. At least the place looked like Seamus' old home. If only Seamus could be the man he's been before.

"I don't have the gold, Uncle."

283

The low-spoken admission seemed to spark his uncle's interest. He lifted his head and pinned Luke with his green eyes. Luke started. The depths of Seamus' eyes were startlingly clear.

"You do not need the gold, lad," Seamus said. "You have her love."

Luke's heart gave a flip. Did he mean Brianna? How could he? Or did he speak of Luke's father and mother again? He didn't think he could bear it.

"Uncle, I…" He leaned closer and placed his hands on the arms of his uncle's chair, his fingers digging into the velvet. "Pray, tell me what you mean."

Seamus laughed, the booming sound Luke had always associated with the man who raised him. His heart beat with cautious hope.

"Love, lad!" Seamus said. "'Tis more powerful than MacDonald gold, I wager."

What was this? Luke opened his mouth to question him further, but Seamus's glorious green eyes clouded. As Luke's spirits sank, Seamus began to rock and hum.

"Where be your bride, Lucas?" he asked in a faraway voice. "She be with those darlin' boys of yours?"

Luke's throat tightened. "Nay, Uncle," he said. "I'm Luke."

The high-pitched laugh Seamus uttered chilled him. Gone again. Luke patted his uncle's hand and stood.

"Mrs. O'Grady?" Luke called.

The lady peeped from the kitchen, her mop cap slightly askew. "Aye, Master Luke?"

"I'm off to the workshop."

She simply nodded. That struck him as odd. He knew it wasn't their custom to work on a Sunday, that the MacDonalds had never done anything after Mass but talk and eat and doze. Luke needed to do something to occupy his mind.

The woman nodded. "Very good, sir."

Luke gazed at his uncle for another moment before leaving the cottage. He was torn; unable to stay with his uncle and unwilling to hear his brothers' questions. Mrs. O'Grady would shoo them out of the kitchen at any moment.

"Bloody beautiful," he muttered.

His uncle said nothing and Luke left. Unexpectedly,

both his brothers were in the workshop. Well, that explained why Mrs. O'Grady had not found it odd that Luke was headed there, too. Patrick and Sean weren't busy. Nay they stood close, talking animatedly. Patrick stabbed at the air while Sean held his hands up in a placating gesture. Luke could well guess the topic of discussion. The bloody gold.

"Hello, Patrick," he said. "Sean."

The younger men each gave a start and turned. Luke easily read the expressions on their faces. Patrick looked angry and Sean looked puzzled.

"Good afternoon, Luke," Patrick returned.

"I thought the two of you were at the cottage." Luke walked over to the back of the shop and leaned against the tall stool near his workbench. "I sat with Uncle Seamus. Ah, he's no better."

"Nay, he isn't," Sean put in. He glanced over at Patrick and swallowed audibly. "We had hoped that… Well, now you be home and all…"

Patrick spat out a curse. "Enough dancin' around it, Sean. Where's the gold, Luke?"

Luke raked his fingers through his hair and blew out

a breath. "I couldn't bring it home, lads. I couldn't."

"What the bloody—!" Patrick said. "Why not?"

Sean grabbed onto Patrick's arm. "Easy, Patrick. We need to be hearin' Luke's side of the story."

Patrick shrugged out of Sean's grip. "His bloody side? Fine."

His eyes bore into Luke's but Luke didn't flinch.

"Tell us, dear brother," Patrick snarled. "What was so important you saw fit to leave our gold in the future?"

Luke kept his gaze steady. "The Pixie needed it."

Patrick snorted. "I knew you fancied the chit. She bewitched you."

"Nay!" Luke said. "Brianna— she didn't take the gold for herself, Patrick."

"Aye, but she be usin' it," Patrick said.

Luke shook his head. "Nay!"

"Tell us, Luke," Sean said.

Luke looked toward Sean and read the younger man's attempt to think things through. One look at Patrick told Luke he would fare well with only the whole truth. Bloody beautiful.

"The child O'Shey kidnapped," Luke said. "She's a

Pixie."

"What? A Faery?" Patrick asked. "You said she was sick."

"Aye, she is," Luke said. "With a blood sickness the doctor there is tryin' to heal."

"So why not barter—?" Patrick asked. "Ah, they don't do things that way in the future, do they?"

"Nay they do not, Patrick," Luke said. "And Brianna is using our gold to pay for the sprite's treatment."

Patrick fell silent, his brows drawn together.

"But what of Uncle Seamus, Luke?" Sean asked softly. "He be needin' that gold."

Luke rubbed his hands over his face and sighed. "I know that, Sean. I couldn't let the child die."

"I didn't know," Patrick began. He shook his head. "Did she use all the gold?"

Luke's shoulders slumped. "Nearly."

"You saw it, then?" Sean asked. "You saw our gold?"

Luke nodded. "Aye. She removed the spell that kept it hidden after O'Shey took the girl."

"Miserable imp," Patrick said.

Luke agreed with his brother's words. "The Ulster clan will see to his punishment."

Patrick's blue eyes clouded. "But to harm a child…"

Luke shivered. "Aye."

"What is she like, Luke?" Sean asked.

"The sprite?" Luke gave a short laugh. "Ah, she be a bonny little lass. Spirited and happy. Uncle will— He would've liked her."

"And Brianna?" Patrick asked, suspicion in his voice.

Luke was silent. How to put into words the miracle that was his Pixie?

"She's beautiful and brave and noble," Luke said.

Sean nodded. "If she used the gold for her sister…"

"Aye," Luke answered. "Never for herself."

Patrick cursed again. "You're moonin' over her! We been here with Uncle these weeks and you've been taking your pleasure—"

"Hush, Patrick!" Luke growled. "The girl is honorable. And so is a MacDonald."

Patrick colored at that. "Aye," he muttered. "But what of Uncle Seamus?"

"God, I don't know." He felt tears prick the back of his eyes. "He was bad today, lads. I don't know how to reach him."

"At least he talks to you," Sean said. His eyes were downcast. "He doesn't notice me or Patrick."

"Aye," Patrick agreed. "Maybe because you look so much like Father... I do not know."

"We'll find a way to help him." Luke straightened. "There must be a way."

"How?" Sean asked in a low voice.

His uncle's words, spoken as clear as any uttered in his life before the gold was stolen, rang in Luke's brain. *Love will keep you when all else is gone.* Was there something to the man's ramblings? Would love be the answer? His brothers wouldn't understand. That was certain. They'd surely think Luke as daft as Daniel O'Shey.

"I don't know," he said again.

The disappointment on his brothers' faces was worse than the anger and confusion of a moment ago. He left the workshop, bound for his cottage. He suspected the girl keeping his place for him would have plenty of his clan's own brewed ale. A fitting way to pass an evening. He doubted the drink would drown out his confusion over what to do about his uncle. And he knew it would do nothing to keep thoughts of Brianna from filling his drunken mind.

Chapter 22

"Luke!" Sean called from outside Luke's door.

Luke's eyes slowly opened. His head ached and his tongue felt like cracked leather. He raised himself from the table—he hadn't made it to his bed, apparently—and groaned.

"Jus' a minute," he mumbled.

He stumbled into his room, tripping over a chair set near the door. He found the chamber pot and grumbled as he relieved himself. No loud and marvelous toilet here, no hot shower to pulse away his headache. Was he now some delicate flower, spoiled by the future's conveniences? He shook his head and the room tilted for a moment.

He splashed his face with tepid water from the washbasin and stalked toward the front door. His little brother took up knocking again, the sound reverberating in Luke's aching skull.

"Cease!" Luke grumbled.

Luke pulled the door open and found Sean standing there, his green eyes alight.

"He asked for you, Luke," Sean breathed. "Uncle

Seamus asked for you."

"Nay, Sean." Luke yawned behind his hand and rolled his shoulders. "Surely he asked for Father."

Sean shook his head, his dark hair wild for a moment. "Nay. He asked for you! He asked if you were back from the future."

Luke's heart began to pound. "What precisely did he say, Sean?" His hangover merely a nuisance now, he pulled on his boots and straightened his clothes. "Did he talk to you?"

"Nay," Sean said. "But his voice was strong when he asked for you. Like it used to be... before."

"Aye. Will Uncle Seamus still be there when we arrive?"

Sean knew full well what Luke meant, and the two brothers hurried through the dell toward Uncle Seamus's house.

"Mrs. O'Grady says he was like usual this morning," Sean said in between breaths. "But then he cleared, like. And then he asked for you. I heard him, Luke. Plain as day."

Luke prayed this meant the man would mend. He

knew in his heart that it would take nothing save a miracle to restore Seamus to his family. Like the medical miracle that was saving Violet. Could he be so lucky as to have two miracles?

They reached the house and Luke pushed open the door. Seamus sat in his chair, his eyes bright and his gaze direct. He held himself straight and tall.

Luke caught his breath. "Uncle Seamus?"

Seamus smiled, a bright expression full of the man himself. "Hello, Luke."

Luke skidded to a stop and reminded himself to breathe. It was foolish to hope, after so much disappointment in the recent past. "Good day, Uncle Seamus." He crouched down in front of his uncle, struggling to keep his nerves steady. "How are you?"

"I'm well, my lad." Seamus peered around Luke. "Did you bring the girl?"

Luke blinked. "What?"

"You mean the gold, Uncle," Sean said from behind Luke. "Did Luke bring the gold?"

The man didn't seem to hear Luke's little brother.

"The girl, Luke," Seamus said. "We need the girl.

God, has it been thirty years?"

"What girl?" Sean asked. "The little Pixie?"

Luke shrugged and put the question to Seamus. "What girl, Uncle?"

Seamus laughed and slapped his knee. "We be needin' Luke's love. Bring the Pixie what took…" He trailed off, his bushy brows furrowed.

"The gold, Uncle?" Sean asked.

Seamus said nothing to Sean, but moved his lips. Luke prayed silently. Let him keep his mind long enough to speak it!

"Bring the Pixie what took…," Luke prompted.

A bright smile wreathed their uncle's face. "Your heart!"

Luke sat back on his heels, his pulse pounding. Seamus withdrew back into his dim mind as he watched, talk of Brianna finished.

"Your Pixie, Luke," Sean marveled aloud. "He said to bring her here."

"Aye." Luke shot to his feet, his heart racing. "Dare I, Sean? Do you think it'll work?"

Sean shrugged. "'Tis worth a try. The good Lord

knows we've tried everything else to bring him around."

Luke barked out a laugh at his brother's answer. He clapped him on the shoulder.

"Aye, 'tis worth a try," Luke echoed. He touched the amber still tied around his neck and it throbbed once in response. "I'll go, Sean. And I'll bring her back."

Luke hurried to his house and changed into his future clothes. His hand shook as he tied the laces on his sneakers and he fisted them. *Pray, let this work.* He stood and took a breath. *Pray, let Brianna accept his love.*

As he walked toward the door, a pounding came again.

"Luke!"

Ah, Patrick. Luke crossed to the door and pulled it finding a fuming Patrick standing there. Luke inclined his head.

"Patrick," he said.

Luke moved to walk past him but Patrick grabbed his arm. "Sean says you be goin' back."

Luke shrugged off his hold. "Aye."

Patrick's brow furrowed. "But, what of us?"

Luke smiled then. Would Patrick understand what

Luke was hoping for? What he prayed would work?

"I aim to bring her back with me, brother," Luke said. "And marry her, if she'll have me."

Patrick's mouth gaped open. Luke wouldn't waste another moment of precious time. He couldn't. He walked past him and toward the clearing, with Patrick following close behind.

"She be bringin' the gold with her?" Patrick asked.

Luke waved one hand through the air. "I'm going to bring the lass here, Patrick. Uncle said nothing of the gold. I don't know if it matters."

That stopped Patrick. Luke continued on.

"What matters then, Luke?" Patrick called.

Luke stopped and turned, unable to keep a grin from his face. "Love, brother. Love."

That shut Patrick's mouth tight. Luke made the clearing and held on to the amber. The spinning, the rushing wind, the twisting in his gut and he was back in his bachelor apartment. He waited several moments for the place to settle and his heart to steady. Glancing about the living room, he knew he wouldn't miss this place. Brianna's comfortable little house, though? Easy, Luke.

No use counting on matters that had yet to reveal themselves.

The clock on the wall told him where she would be. The coffee shop. He tore out of the apartment, bound for a future of a different kind. His future.

***

Brianna went about her work at the counter, smiling on cue as she served the patrons their lunch. With Violet on the mend, she had little to worry about from that quarter. Mrs. Henning would keep all in order until Brianna returned this evening. For another lonely evening. Had Luke only been gone for three days? When he'd gone home that first time, she'd known he would return. Now she knew he wouldn't, and whether he was gone three days or three months wouldn't make a bit of difference.

"Brianna!"

She stilled at the familiar voice. Could it be? She turned toward the door. Luke stood there, hesitancy in his manner. His eyes looked uncertain, his hands held stiff at his sides.

Without a glance at Lori or any consideration of the

customers, she ran from behind the counter and threw herself into his arms. "Oh, Luke!"

He held her tight, as if he would absorb her into himself. She would have gladly have given her breath to stay in his embrace, to feel him holding her forever.

"My God, lass," he rumbled.

She pulled back and stared up at him. "You came back."

A grin tipped one corner of his mouth. "Aye."

She tried to gauge his expression. He looked… hopeful. For what? She couldn't guess.

"What is it?" She took a step back when he released her. "This isn't about the—"

"Nay," he chuckled. "I didn't come back for the gold."

"What? I don't understand."

"I came back for you."

Oh, she wanted to believe him. She swallowed hard. "Luke, I—"

"Marry me, Brianna." He pulled her to him again and touched his forehead to hers. "Come home with me."

She opened her mouth to answer, to shout out "yes!"

299

Suddenly she stilled. "What of Violet?"

"She's welcome. If you think she can travel."

She knew he meant a time jump, and this afternoon the child would see Doctor Noble again.

"She goes to the hospital today, Luke. Then we'll know for sure."

He arched one auburn brow and she welcomed the charm that drew her closer. Her pulse raced and his pull touched her soul.

"I still be needin' an answer, lass."

"Yes!" she cried.

Then she kissed him, right there in the coffee shop.

"It's about time!" Lori called. "Bree's been moonin' over you for days."

Brianna's cheeks heated but she flashed a smile at her friend. She faced Luke again.

"I love you, Luke," she said. "After you left…" She shook her head.

"Aye, lass," he said. "I missed you. I love you, too."

He kissed her this time, a heated caress that curled her toes in her shoes. When he released her, she gazed into his eyes. The love was there, green fire that she would happily feel forever. The honor was also there, the honor she knew to be a part of him. God, she loved him.

She turned and hurried over to Lori. "I… Lori, could you…?"

"Tell Mr. S you're leavin'?" Lori asked with a grin. "Sure, hon."

Brianna reached up on tiptoe and hugged Lori. "Thank you, Lori. You've been a good friend."

Lori sniffled and waved a hand in the air. "Go, Bree."

Brianna untied her apron for the last time and grabbed her purse from the back room. She found Luke waiting by the front door, his body thrumming with impatience. His eyes were dark, his face set, and she felt a rush of awareness. She easily caught his eagerness.

"Come, lass," he said.

He took her hand and she felt a jolt. They stepped out into the bright afternoon together, the sounds and sights of the busy street lost as he grabbed her to him again.

He kissed her until she was limp. "Now?"

Her body screamed for him as her heart had a

moment ago. "God, yes. We just— oh! Violet and Mrs. Henning…"

Luke laughed. "My flat, then. 'Tis blessedly empty."

They hurried to his apartment building, unable to keep from touching each other even as they waited for the elevator. Once inside, he lifted her and she sat on the brass rail bracketing the glass walls. He pressed against her, his jeans rasping against hers as she arched against the window behind her. His mouth trailed over her cheek, her throat, as he began to lift her T-shirt.

* * *

The bell dinged and Luke lifted his head. Brianna was still lost, her eyes closed as she breathed in through parted lips. He'd nearly taken her in the glass-framed elevator! *Control, Luke.* Just for a few more minutes.

He got her into his apartment and banged the door shut behind him. She stood there, one hand pressed against her belly as she glanced around the place. Set against the drab walls and furnishings, she was as bright as the morning sun over the dell. Her shirt was wrinkled, her hair mussed, her mouth rosy from his kisses. Aye, he loved her.

302

"Brianna," he rasped.

She faced him fully, her blue eyes wide. Passion was there. Lust, love, and everything that should be between a man and his mate. Then, she smiled.

The next instant she was in his arms, moving beneath him on the dull beige couch as he peeled off her T-shirt, her jeans. Leaning away from her, he pulled his shirt up and over his head. She let out a little purr and he felt it straight to his groin. Leaning up on her elbows, she watched him. She wore another of those silky garments beneath, outlining her nipples through the soft pink fabric. His mouth went dry.

He lowered himself on top of her, rubbing his chest against hers. She arched and held his head close, stroking her fingers through his hair. He gave her what he craved as he moved his mouth to her breast. Nipping her through the silk, he heard her gasp. Her fingers grabbed his hair again and Luke slipped the garment over her head to puddle on the floor. Daylight streamed through the large window behind the couch, touching her flesh as he longed to, as he would. He lowered his head and took one sweet nipple in his mouth.

"Luke!" Brianna wriggled beneath him. "God, Luke!"

He continued to taste her, to nibble and tease until she was pulling his hair. "Aye, Brianna." He reached between them, touched her silky drawers to feel her damp against his fingers. Trembling, he stroked and felt her passion grow. He'd tasted her before, brought her to her release against his tongue as he'd held her safe in his arms. Today he would feel her throb around his shaft, feel her come apart with him as far inside her as he could be.

He took off his jeans, pausing to drop a kiss on her belly, and then stretched on top of her. The wet silk of her drawers pulled and caressed him, drove him nearly to climax. He heard a soft tear as he removed her panties and soon he was there, at that place he'd longed to be since he'd first seen her. She was pure. He would hurt her. Damn.

"Brianna?"

She opened her eyes and smiled. He nearly spent himself right then, on her belly as before.

"Yes, Luke." She licked her lips. "Please."

In one thrust, he entered her. She cried out, but he couldn't stop, couldn't slow as the blood rushed in his ears. It was like the time jump, all swirling lights and pulsing sound. There was no deafening silence, no suspension of sight and sound now. Now there was only more. More pleasure and more love than he could have imagined.

"Ah, lass…" He reached between them again, stroking where their bodies joined until he began to feel her pulsing around him. Her arms wrapped around his neck and she sobbed against his throat as she found her release. The lamp beside the couch fell over, its bulb breaking with a pop. The curtains fluttered and the TV flashed on, blinking through channels as Brianna sobbed his name.

He let go, released the control he'd held with a thin thread. His climax seemed to go on forever. He moved, shook, and held her close until he thought his heart would burst. Then she touched his face and his heart didn't burst. Nay, it swelled.

He stared down at her. "I love you, Brianna."

Tears spiked the lashes that framed those deep blue

eyes. "I love you, Luke."

Chapter 23

Brianna couldn't believe what had happened. Luke's big body was still stretched on top of her, his green eyes compelling as he brought his lips to hers. He'd begun to move against her, inside her, and she winced.

He kissed her brow. "Did I hurt you?"

God, he was hard against her and she couldn't imagine a sweeter pleasure.

"No, Luke." She placed her hands behind his neck and drew him down to her. "Just a bit before, that's all."

He grinned and she felt his charm. He grabbed the remote and with a click turned off the TV. Then he took her there again, moving as she wrapped her legs around his waist. Blue sparks showed beneath her lids as she neared her second release. She shattered and he growled her name as he came inside of her.

Brianna opened her eyes and glanced around the little apartment. "At least nothing broke that time."

Luke's laugh rumbled from where his head lay in the crook of her neck. "Aye. For we're going to do this quite a bit from now on."

After a few more minutes spent snuggling on the

short couch, they rose and dressed.

"We'll just go and pick up Violet." Brianna tucked her T-shirt into her jeans. She spun to face Luke. "Oh! What will I tell Mrs. Henning?"

"The lady who watched the sprite?" He grinned again and she felt a flutter in her breast. "Use a touch of glimmer on her."

They soon arrived at her house, the place that wouldn't be her and Violet's for much longer. Brianna stopped on the porch, her hand on the doorknob, her mind on the coming meeting with Luke's family. Surely, they blamed her for their Uncle's condition; there was no way for her to escape that. Luke understood. He was Luke, after all. And she knew his heart was hers as sure as hers was his. His family would be a different matter.

Luke placed his hand on her shoulder and she faced him. "'Twill be all right, lass. My family will understand."

How could he read her thoughts? She leaned against the door. "But your uncle, Luke. He's so ill. And it's all my fault."

"'Tis true." He smiled and kissed her. "'Twas Uncle

Seamus who told me to come bring you home."

He reached around and turned the knob, and they entered the house. Violet perched on the couch, a smile on her rosy face. "Luke!" She ran to them and threw her arms around Luke's waist. "I knew you'd be back. Grandmother said so."

Luke glanced at Brianna who just shrugged. He scooped Violet into his arms. "What say you to a visit to my Ireland, sprite?"

Violet looked at Brianna, her eyes clear and bright. "Can we, Brianna?"

Brianna winked at Luke and nodded. "Aye."

***

Luke held tight to Brianna, who in turn got a close grip on Violet. The doctor had declared the child fit for travel. Only this morning the fine Dr. Noble had said a reluctant farewell to Violet and Brianna. Luke hadn't missed the doctor's eyes lingering on Luke's lass. True, he'd saved the sprite with his medicine. Brianna was Luke's. And she saved him with her love.

He told himself that Daniel had jumped with him in safety. 'Twas true, Luke hadn't been aware of the imp's presence at the time. He prayed he could keep the Pixies safe.

The little sprite closed her eyes, bracing herself for the jump. Brianna kissed the child's cheek and stared at Luke for a long moment.

"I trust you, Luke," she said as she closed her eyes.

Luke swallowed thickly. He clutched the amber. "Hold on."

The world spun away and for one heart-stopping stretch of time he heard, and felt, nothing. Was Brianna still in his arms? Was the sprite still safe?

He landed flat on his back with Brianna and Violet sprawled over him. *Thank you, Lord.*

"Oh, my," he heard Brianna sigh.

"That was brilliant!" Violet squealed in his ear.

He opened his eyes and saw the afternoon sun was low in the sky. Violet's beaming face was the next thing he saw. She looked nothing like the pale, wan thing he'd first glimpsed through Brianna's window. Nay, she was bright, perky, and full of Pixie magic.

He turned his head to find Brianna gazing around at the trees around them. Her sister disentangled herself and

bounced to her feet. Brianna shifted and Luke took the
moment to keep her close.

"Luke, let me up," Brianna said.

He held on tight until she at last looked at him.
Knowledge shone in her eyes and she gave him a slow
smile. His body stirred and he brought his mouth to hers.
She was his. He wished for a moment that they could
stay just as they were, locked in each other's arms with
nothing to face more serious than if it were going to rain
in the next few hours. He brought his lips to hers.

"This be your Pixie?" Luke heard Patrick ask.

Brianna gasped as she braced herself against his
chest. They both looked at Patrick, whose scowl was as
dark as the afternoon was bright.

"Hello, Patrick," Luke said.

Brianna stood, busily straightening her hair and
clothes as her cheeks flushed pink. Violet stared up at
Patrick, her eyes round.

"You're Luke's brother?" Violet asked.

"Aye." Patrick began to scowl in the sprite's
direction but, apparently, he couldn't keep a smile from
tugging at one corner of his mouth. "You be the Pixie's

sister?"

"Uh huh!" Violet gave a giggled. "And yours, soon."

Patrick's smile was gone in that instant. "What?" He turned toward Luke. "Luke, you're not marryin' the Pixie who—"

"Aye," Luke cut in. He got to his feet. "Brianna, may I present my brother Patrick?"

Brianna inclined her head and Patrick grudgingly bowed in return. Before Patrick could open his mouth once more, Luke held up one hand.

"Pray, send for Father Lanigan," he instructed. "He's to meet us at the chapel at sunset."

Patrick's mouth dropped open. "You don't mean to marry her?"

Luke shut his brother's mouth with one glare.

"Fine." Patrick gave a curt nod and stalked from the clearing.

"Well." Luke let out a breath. "That was pleasant."

Brianna said nothing but he saw the determination on her face. Her cheeks were pale but he didn't miss the sparkle in her eyes. She wouldn't let Patrick's boorish behavior sway her heart. Lord, he loved the lass!

"Do come on, Brianna," Violet said, trembling with excitement. She tugged Brianna's hand. "Come on!"

Luke took Brianna's other hand in his.

She held herself away from him, once more brushing her hands over her hair and jeans. "Luke, I need to take a shower, or… or a bath, I guess. And I can't marry you in my jeans!"

Aye, 'twould not serve for her to be uncomfortable. And while he thought she looked more than fine in her future clothes, he suspected she wouldn't appreciate his masculine opinion just now. Lord knew she would look wonderful in a dress, too.

"Patrick!" Luke called.

His brother stiffened and turned, his hands in fists at his sides. "What, pray?" he growled.

Luke knew he wouldn't step closer; he hadn't lost the fury clear on his face.

"Send Mrs. O'Grady to my cottage," Luke shouted.

Patrick grumbled something Luke was happy to miss and once more stalked away. Luke turned to Brianna and once more took her hand in his.

"Come, lass," Luke said. "You can bathe at my cottage. And I'm sure Mrs. O'Grady can arrange something for you to wear."

***

Brianna arched one brow at him. She said nothing as he and Violet all but pulled her toward the dell. The place was as if out of a fairytale, which seemed fitting to Brianna. Braunach lived here, and the structures she saw dotting the landscape as they hurried by reflected their pride and workmanship. The cottages were quaint, squat in their lovely yards, with spring flowers dressing the windows and front porches.

"Oh, Brianna!" Violet said. "It's so pretty here!"

Luke winked at Violet and looked at Brianna.

She smiled. "Yes it is, love."

"You'll not mind living here, lass?" Luke asked. "Here with me?"

His words made her heart thump, deep and low. If Violet hadn't held her other hand, Brianna would have thrown her arms around Luke's neck and kissed him senseless. Live here with him? She'd live anywhere with him!

"Your dell is lovely, Luke," she said.

Luke grinned and waved her and Violet ahead of him. "My cottage, lass."

There where the trees parted was the prettiest house she'd ever seen. Thatched roof straight and tight, windows peeking from thick half-timbered walls. There were no flowers near the front door, but a bachelor's home wouldn't have them. It was bright and shiny as the sun on the Cornish coast, though.

"It's brilliant!" Violet said.

Brianna caught the look of pride on Luke's face. This was his home. It would be her home, as well. Suddenly she couldn't imagine living anywhere else.

Luke opened the arched door and waved Brianna and Violet in ahead of him. The place wasn't large, just an open room which served as a gathering room. It was furnished simply, no real decorative touches here either. Brianna looked around the space. Simple dressings for the windows wouldn't detract from the mullioned panes and the rough-hewn mantle above the stone fireplace would be well served with some flowers, maybe some candles. She smiled to herself. She wasn't even Luke's wife yet and she was already redecorating his house.

"What do you think, lass?" Luke asked.

"Luke, this place is just—"

"Hello, Master Luke!" someone called from outside.

Luke turned to the doorway and ushered in a stout woman with a round, smiling face. "Hello, Mrs. O'Grady."

The woman looked at Brianna. "Oh, this must be your bride, sir."

Luke's brows shot up. "Patrick told you?"

"Aye."

"It's very nice to meet you, Mrs. O'Grady," Brianna said. "And this is my sister, Violet."

"Hello, Violet." Mrs. O'Grady ran a hand over Violet's hair. "What a pretty little sprite."

"Thank you," Violet said with a smile.

"Are you feelin' more the thing?"

Violet's eyes rounded. "You know about me?"

Mrs. O'Grady winked in Luke's direction. "Master Luke was worried about you when he came home last, sprite. You and your sister, both."

Brianna felt the warmth, knew that this woman was

as close to Luke as a mother would be.

"You'll help us then, Mrs. O'Grady?" Luke asked.

"Aye, though the lass don't need many fripperies to be a fittin' bride."

Brianna's shoulders eased. This woman's good opinion would go far to ease Brianna's mind. If only Luke's family could accept her as easily as this kindly woman.

Mrs. O'Grady clicked her tongue as she turned to Brianna. "But we don't have much time to get ready."

Luke gave a nod. "I'll leave you ladies to your preparations, then."

Mrs. O'Grady waved an absent hand as Luke took his leave. "Now, to find a proper dress."

Brianna stood still as the woman spanned her waist, her shoulders, and her legs.

"One of the MacGregor girls would be just your size, I wager. And I'm sure one of the Meath children would be happy to lend a dress to our sprite here." She placed her hands on her hips. "You two go into Master Luke's room. You'll find clean water in the basin and fresh toweling. The girl what looks after the place has kept it ready for him."

"Thank you, Mrs. O'Grady." Brianna took one of the woman's busy hands in her. "For everything."

Mrs. O'Grady patted Brianna's hand. "'Tis nothin', lass. Master Luke loves you. Seamus said so."

Brianna's heart skipped. "Luke's uncle? He... he said that?"

Mrs. O'Grady smiled. "Aye. And I saw the way Master Luke looked at you and the sprite. You be part of the family already."

Violet clapped her hands together and Brianna felt herself ease a little more.

By the time she'd washed her face and run Luke's brush through her hair, Brianna's nerves were humming again. The crystal still tucked in her pocket was vibrating gently, as if happy to be here in Luke's dell. She decided to take that as a positive sign and tamped down her apprehensions while she brushed Violet's shining hair. Her sister really did seem healthy again, her cheeks pink and her eyes bright as she chattered on about the dell, Mrs. O'Grady and the coming wedding.

"Luke's brother Patrick has a nice smile," Violet

said.

Brianna found that interesting, since the man hadn't smiled in her direction. She could only imagine what Luke was going through now, breaking the news to the rest of the family. "Yes, love. I hope we see more of it."

Chapter 24

Luke sat at the table in Seamus's kitchen, his hands wrapped around a mug of ale. Icy from the cold box, it soothed his throat. He was dreading the talk with his brothers, but knew there was no way out of it. They both sat with him, their gazes probing.

"Have you seen Uncle?" Sean asked finally.

"Nay." Luke shook his head and took another drink. "I can't bear to see him as he was before."

Sean nodded, his eyes sad. "He's not good, brother. He kept talking about you after you left. About your Pixie."

Luke straightened. "He did? About Brianna?"

Sean shrugged. "Aye, though he didn't use her name."

"I'm marrying her today, Sean."

"Patrick told me."

Luke waited for that flash of anger so often on Patrick's face. Sean didn't look angry, though. Just scared. As for Patrick, he just glowered from his place across the table.

"I can imagine what else Patrick told you," Luke

grumbled.

"So you haven't checked on Uncle Seamus since you've been back?" Patrick asked.

"I can't." Luke glanced at Sean, but that brother had his gaze locked on the table. "Patrick, if he's back to the way he was… Gone, like that. I can't bear it."

Patrick took a breath and sat. "Aye."

Luke had to bridge this distance. He and Patrick were too close for Luke to allow a breach, not when he was about to begin his new life with Brianna.

"'Twill be all right, brother," Luke said.

The fear in Patrick's eyes shocked him. With Sean he'd seen it, as clear as the morning sun. Patrick's anger was always there. This fear, though? "I believe he'll mend."

"You can't be knowin' that!" Patrick dragged a hand across his face. "What if we lose him, Luke?"

Without a thought, Luke grabbed his brother's hand. Patrick clung to him, his shoulders shaking with unshed tears.

"We won't, brother," Luke said. "I won't let that happen."

Patrick pulled back. "How you be doin' that, pray?"

Sean lifted his head, hope clear on his face. Ah, God.

"Uncle Seamus spoke of love, Patrick," Luke said. "I don't know what it means, but I had to risk it."

"You love the Pixie?" Patrick asked.

Sean's gaze was as intent as Patrick's was as they waited for Luke's answer.

"Aye."

Patrick gave a nod and sat back. "Aye," he answered.

"And you think this Pixie can save Uncle Seamus?" Sean asked. "How?"

"I don't know." Luke pushed away from the table and stood. "But I be needing a best man."

Patrick eyed him. "And?"

"Stand up with me, brother?" Luke asked.

Patrick didn't hesitate with his agreement. He stood and wrapped Luke in a hug. Sean laughed softly, the sound short but there nonetheless.

Luke pulled back and grinned. "Come, Patrick. Come, Sean. We have to get ready for my wedding."

When Luke arrived at the empty chapel, the sun was

slanting through the stained glass windows set deep in
the thick walls. The women of the dell must have heard
of the ceremony, no doubt from Mrs. O'Grady. Most of
them were near his uncle's age and had looked after Luke
and his brothers while the boys were growing. Some of
them had no doubt seen to placing pink and yellow
flowers at the altar and white ribbons at the ends of the
hand-rubbed wooden pews. They'd tied the largest bow
on the front pew, the one designated for his family.
Family. Luke's heart sank at the thought. He wished they
could all be there today, his fine parents and his uncle,
sane, whole, and healthy.

He tugged on his cravat and braced one foot on the
nearest pew to buff away a smudge on his boot with his
thumb. Fine MacDonald boots, he thought as he
glimpsed his reflection in the black polished leather.
'Twas true, they weren't sneakers. And true, the shirt was
a far cry from the soft flannels he'd worn in Indianapolis.
As much as he missed his comfortable modern clothes, it
felt good to be in his own once more. Right. Fitting.

He wondered how Brianna fared. If she was as
nervous as he was. Mrs. O'Grady had returned to Uncle

Seamus's house with the suit of clothes Luke now wore, telling him he couldn't see his bride-to-be before the ceremony. She'd assured him the lass was fine, but until Luke saw Brianna's face his heart wouldn't be at ease. As for his uncle…

Luke couldn't think about him without that hollow ache in his heart, deep in his belly. Sean would bring him into the chapel, to at least be present at the wedding if he wasn't aware of it. Again, that stab of longing struck Luke.

Sean entered the chapel then, alone. His fine clothes were rumpled and his face red. Luke's pulse tripped.

"What's wrong, brother?"

Sean's black brows snapped together. "Uncle Seamus be quite agitated, Luke."

Luke's stomach lurched. "Pray, bring him here, Sean. I want him to see my wedding."

"Aye." Sean sniffed as he wiped his nose on the back of one hand. "Though I don't know what he'll see of it."

With his shoulders slumped, Sean left the chapel. Luke shifted from foot to foot as he waited for the priest to arrive. He wondered how Mrs. O'Grady had dressed his bride. He had little trouble imagining Brianna looking anything short of spectacular, and it didn't matter if she'd dressed her in the finest gown or in a simple walking dress. Lord knew he loved how she looked in her jeans and T-shirt. Or in her silky chemise. He smiled to himself. Or in nothing at all.

Patrick entered the chapel, dressed in finery though his face bore little excitement for the coming event. At least he'd agreed to stand up with Luke, as a brother should. A smile would be most welcome, but Luke wouldn't hold his breath. It would have to be enough that Patrick stood beside him, stoically giving his presence if not his true support.

Movement at the door to the chapel drew Luke's notice from his stone-faced brother, and he turned fully to watch as Sean helped a frail Uncle Seamus down toward the altar. Seamus didn't seem to be aware of his surroundings, his eyes downcast and his face slack. His feet shuffled over the wooden floor as Sean supported nearly all of his weight. Here, in the chapel where they so often attended Mass, his uncle looked even less himself than he had in the familiar surroundings of his home. Luke kept his shoulders straight and held his trembling hands behind his back as Sean and Seamus settled in the front pew.

Luke's attention was drawn to the back doors again as a flurry of activity took place. In a flutter of skirts, the women of the dell rushed into the chapel. Chattering and laughing, they preceded the men and the little place was soon full of hopeful well-wishers. Winks and smiles came from these people who had seen Luke grow up, had comforted him when his parents died and had helped Uncle Seamus keep an eye on the three boys as they'd run through the dell.

Sean's eyes brightened a bit as the lively murmurs and laughter filled the chapel, but he never gave up his hold on an oblivious Seamus. Patrick stiffened beside Luke.

"Luke," he heard Patrick whisper.

He looked at Patrick, who leaned his head toward the entrance. Violet entered, a pretty day dress of pink turning her into the Faery sprite she was. Her shining hair was done in long curls held back from her little face. She

beamed a smile at Luke as she neared, and Luke grinned
at his soon-to-be sister. Settling in the front pew beside
Seamus, she swung her legs back and forth with
excitement. She reached for Seamus and touched his
hand. Luke thought he saw a spark of something in the
old man's eyes, recognition or… something. Then Violet
turned away from him to stare at the door and Luke
followed her gaze. Framed in the doorway was his own
Pixie. His Brianna. Everything faded from notice as she
stepped toward him.

***

Brianna nearly lost her footing as her eyes met
Luke's. The little old ladies of Meath had taken evident
pleasure in seeing her ready for her wedding after Mrs.
O'Grady brought her the borrowed dress. One of them
had styled her hair in a charming chignon, using flowers
and pearls to dress her gold locks. And she couldn't deny
that the satin gown, in a lovely shade of pale blue that
matched the crystal key tied around her wrist by a brand
new ribbon, made her feel as if she could've lived in the
past. Or the present? She gave a shake of her head and
focused on the man waiting for her near the altar. It

327

would all work out. He had promised. And she had his word.

Luke was dressed as fine as she had ever seen: a black jacket topped pants tucked into shining boots, a crisp white shirt and neck cloth beneath a vest of green finished his outfit. He was gorgeous and he would soon be hers. Again. A smile teased her lips. Forever.

A little gray-haired priest soon stood beside Luke and his merry eyes helped ease some of her worry as she neared the altar. Luke's brother Patrick stood with him, and he regarded her with solemn blue eyes. Bloody wonderful.

Violet beamed at her from her place in the front pew and Brianna returned her sister's smile. Then she saw him, the reason for all of this. Seated next to a dark-haired young man who could only be Luke's other brother was Seamus MacDonald, frail and haggard, his red hair lank and unkempt. Vacant eyes stared at nothing she could see and her throat tightened. When Luke took her hand and turned her toward the priest, she could focus on nothing but speaking the vows that bound her forever to her Braunach.

The ceremony was a blur, words repeated as the priest instructed, vows given and accepted. As she kissed her husband she heard applause as if from far away.

Luke lifted his head and grinned. "I love you, Brianna."

Brianna felt like singing. "I love you, Luke."

Luke turned her toward his brother Patrick. Patrick took her hand and kissed it, bowing low. Brianna gave a curtsey as she'd always seen the ladies do in those Regency dramas on PBS, and Luke smiled his surprise and approval.

Luke took her hand then and tugged her close. "I want you to meet my uncle, lass."

Brianna looked at Seamus again, seeing little but the shell of the man he must have once been. She felt Luke's pain deep in her own heart. This was because of her. Because of the stolen gold.

"I would love to meet him, Luke," she managed to say.

They approached the pew and Luke's youngest brother hugged the old man's shoulders.

"Here's Luke, Uncle," he said. "And his bonny bride, Brianna."

Seamus smiled, still gazing at a spot somewhere beyond the altar. Sean released his uncle as Luke and Brianna came closer, and Luke took his brother's place beside Seamus.

"I brought her back, Uncle," Luke said. "'The Pixie what stole my heart.' Like you said."

The man blinked, and it seemed to Brianna as if his green gaze cleared. He looked at her and she felt his affection for her. How could that be? Luke eased his uncle to his feet. Seamus held out one shaking hand toward her and she felt his pull. She suspected he had been as charming as Luke in his day. She took his hand and he smiled. It was so different from the vacant expression he had worn when she first saw him, his face now shining.

"Lass?" he asked, his voice hesitant. "Ah, you look like her."

Brianna felt the key at her wrist begin to tremble, the new ribbon tugging her skin as it jumped. She leaned closer and dropped a kiss on the man's rough cheek. He smelled like clover and fresh water, scents she'd already come to associate with this Braunach dell.

To her surprise, Seamus straightened and stood on his own feet, seeming to grow before her eyes as he stood straight before her.

"Brianna?" she heard Luke say beside her.

She took Luke's hand and stood closer to him. It was magic. Her magic. Maybe even *their* magic, hers and Luke's. Whatever it was, it was obvious Luke's uncle was healing before her eyes!

"Ah, children," Seamus beamed at Brianna and she again felt the love she'd glimpsed when he first looked at her. "Ah, Pixie!"

Seamus hugged Brianna, his arms strong and sure. She could feel his love for her. For life. She looked at Luke, who shrugged his shoulders.

His eyes glistened as he swallowed thickly. "Uncle Seamus, I don't—"

"'Tis love, Luke," the man said. He covered Brianna and Luke's joined hands and gave a shout of delight at the chapel ceiling. "Love will keep you when all else is gone."

331

Chapter 25

Luke could hardly believe his eyes. Seamus was as he had been before, strong, tall, and bright. Luke could feel the power pass between their three joined hands, love and magic flowing from Brianna and through the two Braunach like a rainbow through the sky.

He glanced at his brothers and saw their amazement. Hope was there, aye. And confusion that mirrored Luke's own. He felt a laugh bubble in his throat. 'Twas true, amazing though it was. Their love had healed Seamus!

"But how, Uncle?" Luke asked. "I thought your gold was the key."

"The key?" Seamus laughed. "'Tis fitting, boy."

Luke blinked in confusion.

Seamus grabbed Brianna's key where it still hung at her wrist. "'Tis the crystal, boy. The crystal and the amber together."

Luke felt the amber throb at his throat, vibrate as if it wanted to be free of its bounds. He tore off his neck cloth and closed his hand around the stone. With one tug, he snapped the leather holding the amber close to his throat and held the pendant out in front of him. His uncle gently

untied Brianna's key from her wrist, dropping her a wink
as he did so. Oh, the man was well indeed. His charm
was back as sure as his wits. Seamus took the amber
from Luke's fingers and fitted the crystal key into the
center of the stone. In a blinding flash, the key began to
disappear into the amber.

They stared as the key melted into the amber, as
pink, white, and blue light filled the chapel. At last the
stone glowed golden and Seamus held it aloft. It twirled
on the leather cord, as last dimming to its usual amber
shade. Seamus gave a nod of satisfaction, tied it around
his own neck, and placed his hands on his hips.

At last, Luke found his voice. "You're… you're
well, Uncle? Whole?"

"Aye, my lad!" He looked fondly at Brianna before
grinning in Luke's direction. "And 'twas love what saved
me, not our gold."

Luke's brothers stood and approached their small
circle, and when Luke heard the happy chatter from the
pews, he realized the place had gone quiet from the
moment Luke's and Brianna's and Seamus's hand had
joined.

"Love?" Patrick said. "The love between you and the Pixie did all this?"

Sean smiled, a bright expression Luke hadn't seen on his youngest brother's face in months. "Aye, Patrick. Love. Can you fathom that?"

Luke laughed. The power of their love was something Luke had felt from when he first saw her in the coffee shop. To heal? To take what was weak and frail and make it strong again?

Something occurred to him, another who would benefit from the power in this place. He turned to Brianna and saw her eyes widened as the thought occurred to her at the exact moment it did to him.

"Violet," they said in unison.

Luke and Brianna went over to where Violet sat clasping her hands in her lap.

She grinned up at them, her blue eyes wide. "That was brilliant!"

"Aye, sprite," Luke said. He glanced at Brianna before he crouched down and lifted her in his arms. "'Tis not over, though."

Brianna hugged Luke as she wrapped one arm

around her sister's shoulders. Violet gave a gasp and stiffened, finally laughing out loud as Uncle Seamus had.

"Oh, Brianna!" she cried.

***

Brianna's heart beat slowly as she studied Violet. The little girl's cheeks were rosy and her eyes bright, as she had looked so long ago in Cornwall. She was healed as surely as Luke's uncle had been.

"Luke," she said.

"'Tis true, lass." Luke dropped a kiss on Violet's cheek before setting her down gently on her feet. He grabbed Brianna to him and she felt like laughing as Violet had. "And love be the treasure I've been seekin' all along."

"Took you long enough to be knowin' it, lad!" Seamus laughed.

Luke turned to talk to his uncle as Luke's brothers stepped closer to Brianna. She gazed up at Patrick, seeing his eyes were clouded. When he took her hand this time, she didn't feel the cold politeness he'd shown right after her and Luke's vows had been blessed. No, he seemed to be genuinely pleased at the union now. She couldn't

335

summon anger; if it had been possible to meet the person responsible for Violet's illness, she wouldn't have been civil.

"Brianna, I…" Patrick smiled crookedly, his grin much like Luke's though he didn't look as though he smiled as much as his older brother. There was a darkness there, and her Pixie senses picked up a cloud of something—confusion, anger, desperation?—around his heart. She could tell none of this was directed at her.

She took his hand when he offered it. "Yes, Patrick?"

He blinked, and then wrapped her in a hug. "Thank you, Pixie."

Brianna reached up to return the embrace, but when she touched his shoulder, he flinched. That darkness was back, and Brianna could almost taste his fear.

He straightened and fixed that grin on his face again, and she knew he wouldn't tell her about his shoulder or about what haunted him. So she inclined her head and her new brother-in-law stepped away to let his younger brother come closer. Sean not only hugged her but also lifted her off her feet and twirled her around.

"Thank you, lass!" He set her down and kissed her cheek. "Sister." His blue eyes sparkled. "You saved Uncle Seamus."

"Aye, Sean," Seamus said. "Luke's Pixie was the magic we needed."

Luke looked at his uncle, his brow furrowed, and Brianna wondered what was on his mind. "You said something earlier, Uncle. Something about thirty years?"

Seamus shook his head, but Brianna didn't miss the glint in his eyes. There was something there. Hadn't the man known to fit her now-absent key into the amber? Surely, he'd known that all along.

"Not now, Luke." Seamus winked at Brianna, who flushed. It was easy to see where Luke got his charm. "You be havin' a wife to see to," he finished.

Brianna soon found all the MacDonalds' eyes on her, and her flush turned hotter. Her sister looked at them in obvious confusion, her lips pursed.

"What do they mean, Brianna?" Violet finally asked.

Patrick chuckled and turned away as Sean studied a spot on the floor.

"Come, darlin'." Mrs. O'Grady stepped forward and

placed a hand on the little girl's shoulder. "Your sister and Master Luke have to go to his cottage and see to settin' up their house."

Violet looked confused, and then a look of understanding crossed her face. Oh, God.

"You want to kiss Luke," Violet stated. "Alone."

Brianna looked up at Luke, at the passion and love in his deep green eyes. Yes, she did. She wanted to kiss him until he couldn't see straight. "Aye."

While the rest of the family made their way to Seamus's cottage for a celebration without benefit of the bride and groom's attendance, Luke hurried Brianna the short distance to his house. Their house. When she entered and saw his Spartan bachelor furnishings, she paid it little attention.

Luke shut the door and trailed his fingers over the lacing at the back of her borrowed gown, sending any thoughts of shopping and decorating right out of her mind. He spun her to face him and she wanted him out of his fine clothes, wearing nothing but the smile she'd put on his face. She reached up, removed his neck cloth, and began to work the buttons of his shirt free. He shrugged out of his jacked and she pulled the tails of his shirt out of his very tight pants. The bulge in front strained at the buttons, and she couldn't resist touching him through the fabric.

"Ah, lass," he growled. "Give me some time."

She stroked her fingers once more up the hard ridge, watching as his jaw clenched, and stepped back. "Time is what we have, Luke. Plenty of it."

He grinned and ran his gaze over her. "I thought you looked amazing in those jeans, but this dress…"

She tilted her head to one side, the curls one of the old women had created brushing her cheek. "Are you saying you want the *dress*, Braunach? Surely you know it's borrowed."

Luke blinked. "Brianna, what—?"

She reached up and tugged one shoulder free, running her fingers over her collarbone. "Surely you're thinking of the girl who wore this dress, Luke. One of the many in the dell who found you quite to her liking?"

Luke threw back his head and laughed. "If I could remember whose dress that is, I wouldn't be thinking of her right now."

She stepped closer and ran her hands over his chest, reaching beneath to push the shirt off his marvelous shoulders. "A few of the girls in the chapel seemed disappointed to see you married."

Luke rubbed her back, the laces hanging open in the back of her gown as he stroked lower to her bottom. "Ah, none of them had a claim on me, lass." He kissed her neck, her throat. "No one did. Until you."

She let him remove her dress, her chemise and her stockings, as he danced her into the bedroom. Oh, she'd seen the big bed earlier, ignored the flutter in her belly at the knowledge that they'd share the magnificent thing tonight. She glanced at the bright light filtering through the serviceable curtains at the window. Make that this afternoon.

He placed her on the bed and straightened, watching her while he fumbled to remove the rest of his clothes. His breath came fast. Good. He was as affected as she was, and every breath he took expanded that beautiful chest.

Soon he was naked, and she leaned up on her elbows as he stretched out on top of her. His chest brushed over

340

her nipples, sending heat coursing through her. She arched, relishing the answering growl deep in his throat.

"Ah, Brianna…" He finally brought that mouth to hers and kissed her, deeply, sweetly and completely.

She sighed as his lips left hers to trail over her skin. His tongue flicked over the pulse point at her throat, drew another sigh from her lips as she grabbed a fistful of his hair and urged him toward her breasts. Laughing softly, he took a nipple in his mouth and she closed her eyes. His fingers, strong and insistent, found her center and began to pet her. Trembling, her legs fell open, knowing he'd take her there again. To the place only he'd shown her. The place he'd hinted at from that first kiss in the alley behind the coffee shop.

"Aye, Brianna," he rasped, his breath chilling her wet nipple. He kissed the valley between her breasts. "Take your pleasure, lass."

His thumb circled her, drove her higher as his fingers moved in and out. She soared, so close to her climax as she arched toward him. There were no crashes this time, no glass shattering as the climax shook her body. Only her wildly pounding heart and his murmurs of

341

encouragement added to her cries of pleasure. And it was only Luke holding her when she regained her senses.

"In your pleasure," he began softly, coming up to kiss her. "Aye, 'tis true there was never a lovelier sight."

She caught her breath and looked up at him. His eyes were still dark, his breath labored. The hardness pressed to her leg told her the reason.

"Lean back, MacDonald," she said, pressing a hand on his chest. "I want to see you in yours."

***

Luke let his wife take the lead, curious to see what she'd do to him. 'Twas true, just looking at her brought him close to his release. When she began to trail kisses along his throat, his chest, he silently vowed to hold on to some control. Her fingers, light and clever, stroked him, reached down to grasp him. Luke was torn between collapsing on the pillow with his eyes shut to leaning up on his elbows so he could watch as she aroused him to almost painful hardness. When she dropped a kiss on his belly, he chose the latter.

Brianna's hair, once done up as the lasses of his time, now tangled down her back and over her shoulder.

He recalled how she'd thrashed beneath him in her pleasure, how she'd cried out to him as she'd found her peak. God, he nearly spent himself now at the memory. The memory wasn't nearly as incredible as what she did next.

Her tongue flicked into his navel and Luke sucked in a breath. Tossing her hair over one shoulder, she brought her mouth to him. Her lips ran over his flesh, soft and insistent, as he watched her. He could hear his pulse pounding, feel every stroke, every kiss, straight through to his heart. She wasn't as skilled as the harlot in the dell and surely not as the woman who'd put herself in Luke's bed in Indianapolis. But God, Brianna took him where he'd never been before. So close to the edge he could feel each lick, each kiss, on his soul.

Her silky hair trailed over his thighs, her clever hands touched his belly, his shaft, as she closed her mouth over the head. Luke watched as he began to move beneath her, his restraint weakening as she moved her lips over him, up and down, again and again.

"Brianna!" he rasped.

She lifted her head and smiled up at him, her eyes

sparkling. "Aye, Braunach?"

Choking on a laugh, Luke grabbed her to him and kissed her. Urging her on top of him, he began to move against her soft belly. She shifted, cradling his heat with hers, and he clutched her bottom with both hands. Her knees were up against his sides, and she was open. Wide open and wet and hot and he lifted her. With one smooth motion, he was inside.

She gasped as she moved, stroking him as she had with her hands, her mouth. The bed creaked as he matched her rhythm. He turned and pinned her beneath him then, grabbing her hands and stretching her arms up over her head. He was on top now, moving in and out of her as she began to pulse around him. Her legs wrapped around his waist as she met each thrust and he let go of his control.

"Open your eyes, Brianna," he said. "Look at me."

She did, her pupils dilating as their gazes met and held. Love flowed between them, its threads stronger than the passion so thick now. Her eyes closed and she cried out his name.

As she arched beneath him, finding her second

release, Luke drove deeper still. His release tore a cry from him as he poured himself into her.

Brianna was still trembling, each little movement doing amazing things to his shaft buried within her, and Luke leaned up on his elbows and stared down at her. Her skin was damp and flushed, her eyes closed as she panted through parted lips. Her breath was reedy and his was harsh as the evening shadows finally began to spread through the room. Luke kissed her and held her until she came back to herself as his own heartbeat finally slowed.

"Luke MacDonald," she sighed at last. She opened her eyes and grinned. "That charm of yours is going to kill me."

Luke laughed, the sound harsh as he caught his breath. "Nay, lass. 'Twas your charm that brought me to my knees."

She held on to him, with her arms and herself, and Luke knew then that the passion, the magic and the love was tied into one amazing miracle. The miracle he held in his arms.

Chapter 26

The next day, their first full day as man and wife, Luke awoke with an erection. He peered through one heavy-lidded eye to see the reason. Brianna was draped over him, murmuring in her sleep as she rubbed his chest with her hand. And his cock with her leg. She was all soft and pink from sleep, and he eased her onto her back.

"Brianna, lass," he whispered, close to one dainty little ear. "Wake up, Brianna MacDonald."

"Mmm," she sighed. She stretched then, the sheets straining against her breasts. "Brianna MacDonald."

Her eyes snapped open and she stared up at him. "MacDonald!" A lazy smile teased her rosy lips. "G'morning, husband."

Luke kissed the smile from her lips as he found another way to wake her. He caught her sighs of pleasure in his mouth as he found his own release inside of her. 'Twas true, there surely wasn't a finer way to greet the day.

He sat up and brushed his hair back from his face as his wife moved slowly to a sitting position. She yawned behind one hand as she glanced around the room.

"I'm glad there doesn't seem to be any damage when we… When I…"

She flushed and Luke couldn't help laughing. "No broken glass, Brianna? No books thrown from their shelves?"

She laughed with him. "Thank God I don't have to restrain myself around you."

Luke felt pure masculine pride fill his body. "Aye. And 'tis a good thing, if the sprite is going to live with us."

Brianna's brows rose. "Violet will live with us? I hadn't thought about it."

"She is your sister, lass." Luke took her hand. "And my family, now."

The smile she gave him was dazzling. "I know that. You love her as much as I do. I thought she'd want to go back to Grandmother's, though."

Hollowness filled Luke when he thought of Violet clear in the future, let alone in Cornwall. "I suppose I could take her there with Seamus's amber. But without your key?" He shrugged.

Brianna tapped a finger against her lips, her brow

furrowed. "We'll have to ask your uncle, I believe. He seems to know more about all of this than he's letting on."

"Aye." Luke stood at the side of the bed. "And this morning will be a good enough time to learn what all the old man has been hiding."

"Hiding?" Brianna faced him.

Then her eyes ran over his naked form and Luke didn't think about Violet or his uncle's secrets. "If you keep looking at me like that lass, we won't get to Uncle Seamus's cottage much before midday." The grin she gave him shot a spark straight to his groin. "Cheeky lass."

Brianna laughed and hurried past him to duck behind the screen set against one wall. He gave her a few private minutes as he dressed, his mind working. Violet would want to return to her grandmother. And Brianna would want to see the woman as well. Again, he thought of what his uncle had said about waiting thirty long years. However, between the events of yesterday—and last night and this morning!—Luke wasn't as clearheaded as he could be. He laughed to himself. He wouldn't have wanted it any other way.

"Luke, I wondered about your brother Patrick." Brianna stepped out of the dressing room wearing nothing but her chemise from last night. "He seemed… distant. Is he always so shuttered?"

Luke focused on what she was saying, despite the way the linen clung to her sweet body in the pink morning light coming from the window. "Since Seamus got sick, Patrick has been on edge." He walked to the washstand behind the screen and splashed water on his face. "He's always been quick to temper. He used to be just as quick to laugh."

When he stepped back into the room, he saw her disbelieving expression.

"I doubt I'll see that brother's laughter any time soon."

He walked to her and took her hand. "Patrick will love you, Brianna. You saved our uncle and he won't be forgettin' that."

She waved one hand in the air. "I know. There is darkness in him, Luke. I only hope that… Oh, I don't know what troubles him."

"Nor I." Luke recalled something as he finished dressing. "Mrs. O'Grady said she left you some more garments in the dressing room."

In an instant, Brianna was gone through the door at the back of the room. He could hear her murmurs of delight as she found the castoffs the girls in the dell had given her. He'd dress her in finery, just as soon as they had a chance to go to the dressmakers. He'd miss her jeans, though. And the sweet little T-shirts that suited her body so well.

She emerged, a day gown of blue wrapping her figure. A blush colored her cheeks as she stepped closer to him. "What do you think, husband? Will I suit?"

Luke grinned. "Aye."

When they arrived at Seamus's cottage, sounds of talk and laughter drifted out of the front windows. Seamus's deep rumble was paired with Sean's lighter tones and Violet's high-pitched laughter. Luke could feel the delight coming off Brianna as she tugged his hand toward the front door. His own heart was lighter than it had been in weeks.

Luke pushed open the front door to find his uncle in

his favorite chair with Violet perched at his elbow.

"Oh, do have another sweet, Uncle!" Violet giggled.

"Now, sprite," Uncle Seamus said. "'Tis true I'll be as fat as an Ulster Leprechaun if I eat another."

Violet laughed again. When she turned, she spotted them and her face lit with pleasure. "Brianna!" She ran to them. "Luke! I'm so surprised to see you."

"Why, love?" Brianna asked as she hugged her sister.

"Sean said that you and Luke wouldn't show yourselves until tonight, if then."

Brianna's cheeks turned pink again. Aye, but the lass was fetchin' when she blushed.

"We had to see our family, sprite," Luke said. "'Twill be time enough for us to be alone."

Violet shrugged and returned to his uncle's side. She plucked a candy from the bowl on the table beside Seamus's chair. "Mrs. O'Grady makes the loveliest confections, Brianna."

"But there's more substantial offerings in the kitchen," Uncle Seamus offered. "Seems the sprite here wakes with the sun."

"Have you eaten breakfast then, love?" Brianna asked. "Taken your medicine?"

Violet laughed. "I don't need to take that anymore, remember?"

Brianna glanced at Luke and nodded. "True. We'll go eat something, then."

"Hungry, lad?" Seamus teased.

Luke swallowed a grin as he followed his wife into the kitchen. After eating slices of ham and steaming eggs, the two of them returned to the living room. Violet seemed a bundle of positive energy, laughing, skipping, and clapping her hands at something Uncle Seamus had just told her. When the child spotted Brianna, she once more hurried to her side.

"Oh, can we bring Grandmother here, Brianna?" Violet asked.

Brianna appeared confused, but he didn't miss the hope in her eyes. "I don't know, love. Without my key, I don't know if we can find her."

"You can find her, Brianna," Seamus said. "I know these things."

"How, Uncle?" Luke asked.

352

Seamus just winked. Luke was so pleased to have his uncle back and whole that he'd let the secret rest. For now.

"Violet is strong again, lass," Luke offered. "Maybe together you can work your magic?"

Brianna nodded and joined hands with her sister. That blue light he had glimpsed at the hospital back Indianapolis flashed and filled the living room. As Luke watched, unseen wind blew their golden hair about. They closed their eyes and their lips moved in accord, words Luke could barely hear and couldn't recognize. Luke looked at his uncle again and found the man watching the two Pixies with unrestrained satisfaction as his red curls danced about in the air the Pixies stirred. What was the wily old man thinking?

With a resounding pop, a figure appeared in the middle of the room. Clothed in pants of gray topped with a blue sweater, the old woman looked sharp and spry. White hair replaced the gold, but she was undeniably another pretty Pixie. Brianna and Violet parted and the wind that had whipped through the room settled.

"Grandmother!" Violet chirped.

The woman's eyes sparkled as she bent down to hug the child. "You look well, Violet."

The child hugged her grandmother's neck and nodded. "They healed me, Grandmother." She released her and grinned. "Brianna and Luke."

The woman straightened and looked at Luke. "You're the one, then."

Luke saw the same glint of knowledge in her blue eyes he'd seen in Seamus's green ones. What was going on here?

"What are you saying, Grandmother?" Brianna asked.

"The key, love." The woman smiled at Brianna. "It led you to the one to unite the Cornish Pixies and Meath Braunach now."

"Now?" Brianna asked. "But the gold was stolen nearly two hundred years ago."

"Just last month, lass," Seamus corrected.

Luke shook his head in confusion. His manners returned and he bowed to Brianna's grandmother. "A pleasure to meet you, Madam."

"Nonsense, boy." The woman waved at the air and

hugged him tightly. She laughed and turned to Seamus. "Ah, the Braunach. We've tried for generations to get the two together, haven't we?"

Luke's uncle nodded. "Aye, Madam Pixie. Thirty years, by my count. Though I didn't realize how sick I'd become." He turned to Luke. "I'm sorry I troubled you, Luke. You and your brothers."

"We love you, Uncle," Luke said. "We only worried about you."

"But why, Grandmother?" Brianna asked. "I don't understand."

"Over two hundred years ago—" Her grandmother chuckled. "Well, about um… thirty years ago *now,* I think. A Braunach lost his heart when his Pixie fiancée drowned." She sat down on the settee near the hearth and Brianna and Violet flanked her. The old woman put her arm around the child as she patted Brianna's leg. "She was our ancestor, Brianna. Ever since, we've been trying to unite the two clans."

"Thirty years," Luke said. "Wait! 'Twas you, Uncle?"

"Aye, Luke," Seamus said. "I was to wed a Pixie,

but she drowned when the tide trapped her in one of those deep Cornwall caves." He stared at Brianna, an absent smile on his lips. "She was as bonny as your Pixie, too. 'Tis why I never married." He looked at Luke. "Even with my amber I could not make it right. Until now."

"But why now, Uncle?" Luke asked. "Why me?"

"I didn't know it would be you, lad," Seamus said. "I knew when the time was right one of the Pixies would make use of our gold."

Brianna's grandmother took her hand. "You know we've had the MacDonald gold for generations, Brianna. We could only use it in a matter of life and death." She touched Violet's cheek. "And this got both jobs done right and tight. Uniting you to your Braunach and healing our Violet."

"But what of O'Shey?" Luke asked.

Uncle Seamus shrugged. "I don't know how that imp learned of the Pixies, lad. Good that he did, no?"

Luke gazed at his wife, the love of his life, the beat of his heart. "Aye."

"The key, Grandmother," Brianna said. "From the

caves on the Cornish coast. You said it brought more than magic."

"Yes," her grandmother said.

"What, then?" she asked.

Luke grinned as the answer struck him. "Love."

Epilogue

Ireland, 1815

"Papa!"

Luke glanced up from his workbench to see his son barreling toward him on sturdy legs. At nearly four years old, Bryce possessed his mother's blue eyes and his father's auburn curls. However, Luke knew physical features weren't all the child inherited from his parents.

Patrick followed behind the boy, a faint smile on his lips. "Hello, Luke."

Luke nodded to his brother. "Patrick."

In the years since Seamus's illness, the brothers still had not talked about whatever was wrong with Patrick during that time. And while Seamus was his old merry self, Patrick was still guarded, still holding the darkness Brianna said she'd sensed about him. Luke knew today wouldn't be the day Patrick finally revealed what still haunted him.

"Hello, lad." Luke scooped Bryce into his arms. "Where, pray, is your mama?"

"Still with Aunt Violet."

Brianna was back in Cornwall, then. In the future, as it were. Since their marriage, Brianna's own magic had grown more powerful. She no longer needed a talisman like her crystal to travel over time or place.

"'Tis true your mama likes to do her shopping," Luke said.

Bryce wrinkled his nose. "Girl stuff."

Luke laughed. "Aye." He placed his son on the floor and took his hand. "I be finished for the day, I wager." He nodded to Patrick, who turned his attention to his own workbench. "What say we men go pay a visit on Uncle Seamus tonight, Bryce? After your mama comes home."

The little boy's eyes rounded. "Oh, aye! And maybe he can tell me more stories?"

"Stories, pray?" Luke asked.

Bryce clicked his tongue. "Stories, Papa. Like the one about the MacDonald gold."

Luke hid his smile. Seamus liked to regale the boy with tales of stolen gold and how that gold finally united a Braunach to his Pixie. 'Twas true, that was one story Luke could listen to again and again.

"What about Indianapolis, Bryce?" he asked. "You

don't want any tales of that place?"

That turned the boy's attention. "Oh, aye! When can we go there again, Papa?"

Luke laughed again. They waved good-bye to Patrick and made their way back home. When they arrived, Brianna stood in the middle of the living room. Luke's Pixie turned from glossy bags piled on the settee, bags bearing names he now recognized as being from the finest stores in London. Thank God, their gold was restored soon after Seamus's sanity. It had reappeared as if never being gone. And since Luke knew better than to question the fates, he'd simply accepted it. Besides, what was gold when compared to his other treasures?

Brianna hugged their son to her, dropping kisses on his curls. She straightened, fixing her gaze on Luke. That warmth filled his body and, as always, his heart. He held her close, bringing his lips to hers for a sweet kiss, but Bryce wedged himself between them.

"What did Aunt Violet say, Mama?"

Brianna laughed and ruffled the boy's hair. "She said to get ready for another magic lesson when she comes at Christmas, love." She reached into her pocket and withdrew a small pouch of deep blue. "And Great Grandmother sent you this."

Bryce's mouth gaped as she withdrew a crystal key from the pouch. When his small hand closed around it, a crackle of blue light filled the room. Luke knew what that light meant. Pixie magic.

"Brilliant, Mama!"

With that, Bryce ran off toward his bedroom.

"Violet is well, then?" Luke asked Brianna.

"Yes," Brianna said. "You mustn't worry over her."

Luke shrugged. "'Tis a hard habit to break, lass."

She wrapped her arms around his neck and snuggled closer. "You're a good man, Luke MacDonald."

He gave her a squeeze. "I'm a happy man, Brianna."

He thought for a moment of all that had happened since his uncle sickened. Of the honor that had sent him searching for his family's gold. Of the magic that had brought him to Brianna. However, worth more than all of that was the love he'd found. Uncle Seamus had been right. Love had more value than all the gold in Ireland. And Luke would treasure Brianna's love forever.

About the Author

JoMarie DeGioia is a bestselling author of Historical and Contemporary Romance. She's known Mickey Mouse from the "inside," has been a copyeditor for her tiny town's newspaper, and a bookseller. A hybrid author, she also writes Young Adult Fantasy/Adventure stories, New Adult Romance and Paranormal Romance. She gets lost in DIY projects around the house and works out plot ideas during long runs. She divides her time between Central Florida and New England.

Discover books by JoMarie DeGioia

The Dashing Nobles series, including

More Than Passion

Pride and Fire

Just Perfect

More Than Charming

The Cypress Corners series, including

Finding Harmony

Taming Jake

The Gifted YA Fantasy/Adventure Trilogy,

including Gifted

Connect with me online

Twitter: https://twitter.com/JoMarieDeGioia

Facebook:
https://www.facebook.com/JoMarie.DeGioia.Author

Website: www.jomariedegioia.com

www.ingramcontent.com/pod-product-compliance
Lightning Source LLC
Chambersburg PA
CBHW070635180626
46817CB00006B/2131